DWIGHT D. EISENHOWER

Illustrated by Meryl Henderson

DWIGHT D. EISENHOWER

Young Military Leader

by George E. Stanley

ALADDIN PAPERBACKS ·

New York · London Toronto Sydney

ALADDIN PAPERBACKS
An imprint of Simon & Schuster Children's Publishing Division
1230 Avenue of the Americas, New York, NY 10020
Text copyright © 2006 by George E. Stanley
Illustrations copyright © 2006 by Meryl Henderson
All rights reserved, including the right of reproduction in whole
or in part in any form.
ALADDIN PAPERBACKS, CHILDHOOD OF FAMOUS AMERICANS,
and colophon are trademarks of Simon & Schuster, Inc.
Designed by Lisa Vega
The text of this book was set in New Caledonia.
Manufactured in the United States of America
First Aladdin Paperbacks edition June 2006
2 4 6 8 10 9 7 5 3 1
Library of Congress Control Number 2005936020
ISBN-13: 978-1-4169-1257-6
ISBN-10: 1-4169-1257-6

ILLUSTRATIONS

CONTENTS

DWIGHT D. EISENHOWER

Dark Days in Texas

On the night of October 14, 1890, a loud clap of thunder shook the little white house at the corner of Lamar and Day Streets in Denison, Texas, just as David Eisenhower ran to the bottom of the stairs and shouted, "James! My wife's gone into labor! Go get the doctor!"

David had to shout a second time, over more thunder claps, before James Redmon, the boarder who rented a room on the second floor, appeared on the landing.

Redmon was a freight engineer for the Missouri, Kansas & Texas Railroad, a railroad affectionately known as the Katy. He had only been home less than an hour after an all-day run from Kansas City.

David hadn't realized that Redmon had already gone to bed, but he didn't want to leave his wife, and he was sure Redmon wouldn't mind helping him.

"What's the matter, David?" James called downstairs.

"Ida's gone into labor," David repeated. "Would you go get the doctor for her?"

"Of course!" James said. "Just let me get my shoes on."

Outside, the wind had begun to howl. The rain came down in horizontal sheets and rattled the windows of the little house. It sounded like drums in a Fourth of July parade, but even that couldn't drown out the sound of one of the Katy freight trains as it roared past.

David Eisenhower hurried back over to the door of the bedroom. His wife was now surrounded by several women from the neighborhood.

That was one thing about this town, David thought: No matter how down and out you were, no matter how lowly your job, people would come to your aid whenever you needed them.

Just then, a fully clothed James Redmon bounded down the stairs, grabbed a hat and a coat from the rack by the door, and headed out into what David was sure was one of the worst thunderstorms they had had that year.

For several minutes, David paced around the living room, then he leaned up against a wall and thought about the world his third child would be born into. How had his life come to this miserable point in just two years? he wondered.

If he hadn't decided to quit his job at the Eisenhower family's general store in Hope, Kansas, things would be different, he was sure. David had grown so tired of selling supplies to the local farmers that he couldn't stand it anymore. His family thought he was irresponsible to leave Hope and his job, with a wife and a second child on its way, but David knew that if he had stayed in Hope, he would only have gotten more depressed.

David's brother, Abe, agreed to take care of Ida and their son, Arthur, while David traveled down to Texas to look for work. He found it in Denison, cleaning train engines. He only earned ten dollars a week, but at least he could rent a room in a boarding-house close to the railroad yards. If he lived frugally, he could make ends meet, but he wasn't prepared for the loneliness he experienced.

In January 1889, David received a letter from Ida telling him that he had a second son, whom she had named Edgar, after her favorite writer, Edgar Allan Poe. That was followed the next month by a letter from his father telling him that he had decided to sell the general store and move his own family to Abilene, Kansas. Within weeks, David received yet another letter, this time from his brother Abe, telling him that he was disposing of his veterinary business in Hope and was planning to move to Abilene, too.

David didn't want to admit that the news from Abe depressed him, but it did. With his whole family leaving Hope, David had to make a decision about his wife and two sons, whom he knew he could barely support on his salary. After much soul searching and discussions with other railroad workers, though, he rented a tiny, wood-frame house beside the Katy railroad tracks and moved his family to Denison.

Although soot from the passing trains coated the house and everything else in its vicinity, it did have an upstairs room, which David was able to rent out. This brought in enough extra money that he felt the family could not only survive but have enough left over for a few occasional luxuries, such as the six hot tamales that Ida bought weekly from a local peddler for five cents.

Things were actually beginning to look up for the four of them, David thought. However, things changed in June when a telegram arrived from Abilene with the news that his mother, Rebecca, had died.

The guilt David had initially felt at having left his parents and brother behind in Kansas swiftly returned. Taking four-year-old Arthur with him, he left Ida, who was five months' pregnant at the time, and one-year-old Edgar, and returned to Abilene.

At the funeral, David thought of trying to find work in Abilene so he wouldn't have to leave his father and brother behind yet another time, then sending for Ida and Edgar. However, after partaking heartily of a bountiful meal prepared by the ladies of the River Brethren Church, David realized that doing that would only be seen by the family as yet another act of foolishness, much as his leaving Kansas for Texas two years earlier had been. He didn't want to see the disappointment in the eyes of his relatives again.

The summer of 1890 was extraordinarily hot in Denison, but since the Eisenhowers' house was so close to the railroad tracks, the yard was a dangerous place for Arthur and Edgar to play. Instead, the two boys spent much of their time playing by an open window until one of the frequent trains came rushing by. When that happened, it was Arthur's job to close the window as fast as he could so that the soot that covered the outside of the house wouldn't find its way inside. On the days when Ida was feeling up to it, and even on a few days when she wasn't, she would take the boys to a nearby park so they could all cool off under the shade of the big old elm trees.

Even though the family had little money, Ida and the two boys made the best of their situation, but David continued to be unhappy. The only bright spot in his life—and in Ida's, when she would admit it—was the thought that their third child might be a girl. With two boys already, David and Ida wanted a girl more than anything else in the world.

Suddenly, a clap of thunder and a flash of lightning so bright that it turned the inside of the little house to daylight brought David back from his memories.

Seconds later, Ida screamed.

David rushed to their bedroom door, but he was stopped by Mrs. Gentry, a woman twice his size, who kept a couple of milk cows in her backyard and sold butter in the neighborhood.

"Now, just where do you think you're going, Mr. Eisenhower?" Mrs. Gentry demanded.

"I heard my wife scream," David said, "and I need to see if she's all right."

Mrs. Gentry lifted her face to the ceiling,

moved her lips in what David was sure was a silent prayer, then brought it back down and looked David straight in the eyes. "Of course, she's all right, Mr. Eisenhower," she said. "As all right as a woman can be when she's giving birth."

"I've sent Mr. Redmon for the doctor," David said, trying to keep the panic out of his voice, "and I'm sure it won't be long until—"

Another scream from Ida stopped the flow of words coming out of David's mouth, and he looked into the bedroom over Mrs. Gentry's shoulder.

"Some of the women with your wife have given birth to six and seven and even more children, Mr. Eisenhower, so they're not going to be too terribly concerned if the doctor doesn't get here on time," Mrs. Gentry said. "There's nothing to worry about. Childbirth is a natural thing, sir, and the good Lord gave us women the strength to get through it without any help from you men."

"Still—" David said, but whatever else it was that he'd planned to add to his argument was halted by a baby's loud wail.

"Oh, my goodness!" one of the women in the bedroom shouted. "The Eisenhowers have another healthy boy!"

David was sure that the brief flash of disappointment on his face must have been evident to Mrs. Gentry, but she didn't remark on it. Instead, she went back into the bedroom and closed the door behind her.

David walked to the opposite side of the room and leaned up against the wall again, feeling it suddenly vibrate as another freight train roared past their house.

David wasn't exactly sure how much later it was when James Redmon returned with the doctor. The two figures, soaked from the thunderstorm still raging outside, stood for just a minute in the gloom of the entryway.

Redmon, finally spotting David, said, "Did something bad happen?"

"No, the women delivered the baby," David replied, "and there were no complications."

"I'm sorry we didn't get back here in time for the birth," Redmon said, "but the doctor can take care of the rest of it."

David nodded and showed the doctor to the bedroom door. Turning back to Redmon, he said, "You need to go on upstairs and get some sleep. Don't you have the San Antonio run tomorrow?"

Redmon grinned. "I sure do, and I'm looking forward to seeing Dolores when I get there too," he said. "If she'll have me, I may just ask her to marry me this time."

"Is she the one you showed me a picture of?" David asked.

Redmon nodded. "She's a beauty, isn't she?" he said.

"She is at that," David replied, "but do you think she'll want to move up here to Denison?"

Redmon shrugged. "I don't know, but it

really wouldn't make any difference to me, because I've been thinking about transferring down to San Antonio, anyway." He yawned. "I think I'll hit the hay, but if you need me for anything else, David, just come knock on my door and I'll get up again."

"Thanks, James," David said.

As he watched Redmon ascend the stairs to his room, David's only thoughts were about whether he'd be able to find another boarder as reliable as the one he had now. With the new baby, that income would be absolutely essential, because now there would be even less money to go around.

All of a sudden, almost as if he could no longer control it, David's head turned to look at the front door. To most people, it was merely a piece of wood with a small pane of glass in it, but now David saw it as a way to escape from his troubles.

It would be so easy, David thought, *to open that door and go back to Kansas, and then, after I found a decent job, send for Ida and the boys.* He stopped and broke out in a sweat that sent rivulets of perspiration from his brow into his eyes and from his neck down his back. "I can't keep doing this," David whispered. "I can't keep running away."

Just then, Mrs. Gentry opened the door of the bedroom and let the doctor out.

"Ah, Mr. Eisenhower," the doctor said. "You've got a really healthy son in that one."

"Thanks, Doc," David said. "How's my wife doing?"

"Oh, very well, very well indeed, sir," the doctor said. He leaned up close to David and whispered, "The ladies of this town do such a great job when it comes to birthing a child, that one of these days I'm sure they'll forget to call me."

David smiled.

"I'll come by tomorrow and check on both your son and Mrs. Eisenhower, but for now, I think I'll go on home," the doctor said. "This has been a busy night."

Several of the ladies followed the doctor out the door, all whispering their congratulations to David and assuring him that they were available for Ida anytime she needed them.

"Thank you all very much," David told them. "I can never repay your kindness."

"We wouldn't be neighbors if we didn't help out when we were needed," they all told him.

"Mr. Eisenhower," Mrs. Gentry called from the bedroom door. "Mrs. Eisenhower wishes to see you."

David hurried into the bedroom. A single candle was burning on a small table in the corner. It was the only light, but it was easy for David to see that Ida's face, though pale, was also showing a mother's pride.

"Come look at your new son, David," Ida whispered.

14

David approached the side of the bed, wondering just what he'd see in this new baby that he hadn't already seen in the other two, but the minute he set eyes on its face, he felt a change come over him. It wasn't just in how he felt about the child, but about how he felt about his family. For what seemed almost the first time in his married life, he wondered how he ever could have left them for more than just a few hours at a time.

"What do you think of him, David?" Ida asked.

"I think he's beautiful," David said tearfully and, as he turned his head to look at his wife, he added, "and so are you, my darling wife."

"His name is David Dwight Eisenhower," Ida said. She looked up at her husband. "I wanted him to have both your name and Reverend Dwight Moody's, because his spiritual messages have given me so much hope these last few years."

• • •

A few weeks later, after people began calling the baby Dave instead of David, Ida switched his first and middle names. He was now called Dwight. In the family Bible, though, his name remained David Dwight Eisenhower, because Ida had written it in indelible ink.

Over the next few months, somehow, with the help of friends and many prayers, David's salary with the railroad managed to feed and clothe the five of them, but barely. Luckily, James Redmon didn't move to San Antonio as planned, so the money from his rent remained part of the Eisenhowers' income.

In the spring of 1891, David's father, Jacob, came to Denison for a visit. He had hoped it would be a happy trip, but it turned out to be a sad one instead. The sense of gloom David and Ida and the boys felt at being so far away from Abilene and the rest of the Eisenhower family was all anyone could think about.

When Jacob returned home, he immediately asked other members of the family to write David and Ida and suggest that they return to Kansas. David always wrote back telling them that without the prospect of a job to support his family, he'd have to stay in Texas and continue to work for the railroad.

Finally, one day, a telegram arrived from Chris Musser, the foreman of the Belle Springs Creamery in Abilene. JOB AWAITS YOU, it read.

David looked up at Ida, who was standing in the middle of the living room, surrounded by Arthur, Edgar, and Dwight, all three clinging to her skirt as a passing freight train shook the house.

"We're going home!" David shouted to them. "We're going back to Kansas!"

Return to Kansas

"What do you think?" David asked Ida and the boys.

It was late spring, 1891, and they were all standing in front of a tiny house, barely more than a shack, two blocks south of the Union Pacific Railroad tracks in Abilene, Kansas. The front yard was full of weeds, but the backyard had a wooden fence around it, and there was a shed for wood and coal not far from the rear of the house.

"I think it's beautiful," Ida said. She looked down at Arthur, Edgar, and Dwight. "If we can afford the rent, boys, this will be our new home." Looking back up at David, she asked, "Can we?"

Before his father could reply, one-year-old Dwight said, "Play!"

"We don't live here yet, Dwight," Arthur said. "We'll have to wait to do that until we move in."

"When will that be, Mama?" Edgar asked.

"Soon, I hope," Ida said. She looked back at David. "Can we afford it?" she repeated.

David put his hand in his pocket and pulled out a wad of bills and coins. "This is all we have, Ida. Twenty-four dollars and fifteen cents," he said, "but, yes, I think we can afford it."

"Oh, David, why are you carrying around that much money?" Ida said. "It should be in the bank."

"I'll put my first paycheck from the creamery in the bank, Ida," David promised, "but we'll need most of this to rent the house and buy some groceries."

"Could we at least peek in the windows,

Papa?" Arthur asked. "I want to see what our room looks like."

"I think that's a good idea, too, David," Ida said. "I want to decide against which wall I'm going to put my piano."

"*Piano?*" Dwight said.

"You know what a piano is, Dwight," Edgar said. "That's what Mrs. Collins played in Denison at church, so we could sing all those hymns."

Ida let out a contented sigh. "I'll finally be able to have my ebony piano again," she said. "I have missed it so much."

"There are a lot of things we've missed these last few years, Ida," David said, turning a slow circle as he surveyed the neighborhood, "but now that we're back in Abilene, with family, I just feel that all is right with the world. So yes, let's go take a look."

Three days later, final arrangements were made to move into the house on Second

Street, after David had begun work as a maintenance engineer at the Belle Springs Creamery. His job was to ensure that the machinery and the steam equipment were in good working order. Although he was making more money now than he had in Denison, it wasn't that much more. Ida was expecting their fourth child. They'd soon have another mouth to feed, but even that didn't seem to bother anyone, least of all David. He was so happy to be back in Kansas that he never complained about anything.

Dwight was excited about the new house. Since it wasn't as close to the railroad tracks, he could play outside more. But what he enjoyed most was when his brothers took him all over Abilene.

One morning, Ida awakened Arthur and whispered, "It's wash day, son, and I know you boys always help me, but a couple of the ladies from the church are coming by to give me a hand with the laundry in exchange for piano lessons. I was hoping that you could take Edgar and Dwight downtown."

"All right, Mama," Arthur said enthusiastically. He had already jumped out of bed and was starting to get dressed. "I honestly don't mind helping you with the laundry, but I like looking around Abilene, too."

"Thank you, Arthur. Thank you very much," his mother said with a smile. "You're a wonderful son and a great comfort to me and your father."

After breakfast, just as Arthur, Edgar, and Dwight headed out of the house, Ida stopped Arthur and handed him some pennies. "That should be enough for ice cream," she said.

"Oh, Mama!" Arthur said. "Thank you!"

When the three boys reached the corner, Arthur said, "If you're both good, I'll buy you each an ice-cream cone."

"You'll buy them, anyway, Arthur," Edgar said. "I saw Mama give you that money, and she didn't say anything about our being good!"

"Well, I'm telling you that you have to be good," Arthur countered.

"I'm good," Dwight said.

Arthur grinned. "Yes, you are, Dwight," he said.

As the three of them got closer to downtown, they were able to walk on sidewalks made from wooden planks, instead of on dirt.

"Wild Bill Hickok was once the marshal of Abilene," Arthur said. "The people in the town hired him for the job because Abilene used to be a really rough place to live, Papa said."

"I want to see his gun," Dwight said.

"You can't now, Dwight," Edgar said. "Wild Bill Hickok doesn't live here anymore."

"Where did he go?" Dwight asked.

"He joined Buffalo Bill Cody's *Wild West* show," Arthur said. "When we were living in Denison, Papa was going to take us to Dallas to see the show, but we didn't have enough money for the tickets. I don't think Wild Bill Hickok was still in the show, anyway."

Suddenly, a loud whistle sounded, and Dwight covered his ears.

"Come on!" Edgar shouted. "It's a fire!"

Up ahead, they saw men running out of the stores, heading north. Just then, a horse-drawn fire truck rounded a corner and headed in the direction the men were running.

"It's probably some rich person's house that's on fire," Arthur said.

The Eisenhower boys knew that the people of Abilene who had the most money lived in the north part of their town.

"Well, they may be rich for Abilene, Arthur, but Mama said they're not as rich as the people in Topeka," Edgar said, "so I'm not impressed with them."

"What's a Topeka?" Dwight asked.

"Topeka is the capital of Kansas, Dwight," Arthur said. "We have a lot of relatives who live there."

"Mama said that Topeka has all kinds of things that we don't have in Abilene yet,"

Edgar added. "They have paved roads and sewers, and water that comes through a faucet in your house."

"I want to go there," Dwight said.

"Nobody's going to Topeka now, Dwight. We're just going to see what's on fire," Edgar said. "Anyway, Arthur and I will get to go before you do, because we're older."

"I smell smoke," Arthur said. "The fire must be close by."

Just as the boys started to cross the street, they had to jump back. A mule-drawn streetcar that provided Abilene's public transportation came racing toward them.

"There's the fire!" Edgar shouted, pointing to his left. "Come on!"

They raced toward a crowd of people who were watching the firemen spray water on the blaze.

"It's Mr. Koenig's butcher shop," Arthur said. "That's where Mama buys meat when we can afford it."

"I guess we won't get to eat meat anymore," Edgar said. "And I really liked those ham bones Mama got there to put in the beans, too."

"She'll just go to another butcher, Edgar, until Mr. Koenig rebuilds his store," Arthur said. "Abilene may not be as big as Topeka, but it has more than one butcher shop."

Just then, Theodore Jackson, Abilene's one policeman, started toward them with his hand raised in the stop sign. "You boys don't want to get any closer," he said. "Some of the folks down there have already been burned by embers, and I'm trying to get them to leave the area."

"Yes sir, Officer Jackson," Arthur said.

"Did it burn everything in the store?" Edgar asked.

"Almost," Officer Jackson said. "But it was the best-smelling fire we've ever had in Abilene, I can tell you that."

"What do you mean?" Arthur asked.

"All that roasting meat," Officer Jackson explained. He grinned at them. "It was all I could do to keep some of the folks from going in there and having a picnic."

Arthur and Edgar laughed.

"I'm hungry," Dwight said.

"Mama gave us some pennies to buy ice cream, Dwight," Arthur said. "We'll go to the drug store in a minute."

"All right," Dwight said.

"Well, I'd better be getting along so I can make sure that the good citizens of Abilene stay out of trouble," Officer Jackson said.

The boys watched as Officer Jackson continued on down the street, then Edgar said, "Are there a lot of people in Abilene who cause trouble, Arthur?"

"Not as many as there used to be," Arthur said as they headed in the direction of the drugstore. "Papa said that the people of Abilene are now mostly plain-speaking pioneers who believe in God and hard work."

"What about the carnival people who live near us?" Edgar asked. "I think they're mostly lazy, and I never see them in church. I've heard they like to fight a lot too."

Arthur shrugged and opened the front door of Brady's Drugstore. "Well, I'm not afraid of them," he said, "but I'm not going to try to pick a fight with them, because those carnival people know how to use knives."

"I'll fight any one of them who tries to pick on me!" Edgar assured him.

"Me too!" Dwight added.

Now that they were suddenly surrounded by the wonderful smells inside the drugstore, though, all talk about fighting was forgotten. They headed toward the back, where Mrs. Brady seemed to be waiting for them.

"My, my, if it isn't the three Eisenhower boys, and they look as though they only have ice cream on their minds," Mrs. Brady said cheerfully. She waited until they were sitting on the soda fountain stools in front of her before she added, "What's it going to be today, gentlemen?"

"Chocolate," Arthur said.

"Strawberry," Edgar said.

"Vanilla," Dwight said.

"I see in front of me three young men who know their minds very well," Mrs. Brady said as she started scooping the ice cream for the cones. "That's a good trait to have."

Just then, a woman came in, trailed by two girls in pigtails. When the Eisenhower boys turned to look at them, the girls stuck out their tongues and started to giggle. Then they turned up their noses and pinched them with their fingers.

"Why are they doing that?" Edgar whispered to Arthur.

"They live in the north part of Abilene and they think they're better than we are," Arthur replied as he took another lick from his cone.

"They're not better than me," Dwight said.

Arthur grinned at Dwight. "No, they're not, and don't you ever forget that, either."

An Important Lesson from a Goose

For the next three years, Dwight stayed in the shadow of both Arthur and Edgar, who thought it was their job to tell him how to do everything, but Dwight never complained. He loved both of his brothers and looked up to them. At the time, it never occurred to him that he really had any say in what he did or didn't do when they were together.

But in late September 1895, just a few weeks before Dwight's fifth birthday, that all changed.

One morning, his aunt Minnie, his

mother's sister, stopped by the Eisenhowers' house and said, "I'm taking Dwight with me to Topeka, Ida, because I want him to meet the rest of the family."

Dwight was so surprised, he didn't know what to say, but he could tell by the expressions on the faces of both Arthur and Edgar that they weren't too happy about it. They waited until their aunt Minnie left, though, before they voiced their complaints.

"Why does Dwight get to go to Topeka instead of us?" Arthur asked.

"We're older than he is, Mama," Edgar added. "We're the ones who should go."

"It was your aunt Minnie's decision, boys," Mrs. Eisenhower said, "and you're not to question what adults do."

Actually, Dwight had wanted to know too. He also had thought that either Arthur or Edgar would go on a trip like this before he would, mainly because they had told him that was what would happen. It never occurred to

Dwight to believe otherwise. Now he had started to think that perhaps his two older brothers didn't know everything. He didn't know how to respond to that, though. In a way, it made him happy, because now he could start making his own decisions about some of the things in his life, but at the same time, it hadn't always been bad having two older brothers to do that for him.

The entire Eisenhower family went to the station to see Dwight and Aunt Minnie off for the trip to Topeka.

"I wish we were all going," Dwight told everyone, "but I'll remember everything I do and I'll tell you all about it when I get back."

"Well, I think that's a wonderful idea, son," Mrs. Eisenhower said. "We'll all be looking forward to that."

Dwight kissed his mother good-bye, shook hands with his father, Arthur, Edgar, and three-year-old Roy. Then he took Aunt Minnie's hand, and they climbed aboard the train that would take them to Topeka.

After they left the station, Dwight craned his neck as far out the open window as he could, until he could no longer see his family standing on the platform.

"You'd better close that window, Dwight," Aunt Minnie finally said. "If any of those embers from the engine come flying in through it, we'll both be covered with soot and your Uncle Luther might not recognize us."

Dwight closed the window quickly and sat down in his seat next to Aunt Minnie. "May I ask you a question?" he said.

"Well, of course, Dwight," Aunt Minnie said.

"Why did you choose me to go with you to Topeka instead of Arthur or Edgar?" Dwight asked.

Aunt Minnie smiled. "I was wondering when that would come up," she said. "Well, you're the middle child, Dwight, and middle children seem to get lost sometimes. I should know. I was one, too. Arthur and Edgar tease you and boss you around a lot, and your mother is still busy with little Roy, and, well, I can tell in her eyes that she's still not gotten over losing baby Paul in March. I thought I'd take you with me to Topeka so you could be special for a few days. Arthur and Edgar can take care of themselves, and now your mother just has to concentrate on taking care of Roy."

At the mention of Paul's name, Dwight had felt his heart skip a beat. He still found himself forgetting that the crib in his parents' bedroom was empty. Paul had lived for a year, and he always had a smile on his face, until toward the end of his life. Then suddenly, on March 16, Paul went away to be with the Lord, the boys were told.

Dwight leaned his head against Aunt Minnie. He loved the way she smelled and felt. There were times when he wanted his mother to sit this close to him, too, but someone else was always trying to get her attention, and he never managed to do it very often.

Dwight felt his eyes getting heavy, not only from the heat of the coach, but from the *clickity-clack* of the train wheels on the rail. He closed his eyes, thinking he would just rest for a few minutes, because he didn't want to miss seeing the countryside between Abilene and Topeka. But the next thing he realized, Aunt Minnie was shaking his shoulder gently and whispering, "Wake up, Dwight. You've been asleep for almost four hours, and we're already in Topeka."

Aunt Minnie's husband, Uncle Luther, was at the railroad station to meet them.

"Welcome to Topeka, young man," Uncle Luther said, shaking hands with Dwight. He kissed his wife and added with a chuckle, "I'm finally going to get a good home-cooked meal after all these weeks."

"You know how to cook, too, Luther," Aunt Minnie scolded him. "Don't go pretending that you've been starving."

Uncle Luther looked down at Dwight and grinned. "I'm in trouble now," he whispered.

When Aunt Minnie and Dwight were in the buggy, Uncle Luther untied the reins from a hitching post, and they started toward their farmhouse, several miles from Topeka.

Dwight gazed eagerly at the unfamiliar scenery. "There are more trees here than in Abilene," he said. "I wish we had this many back home."

"Well, there are a few more, you're right, son," Uncle Luther said, "but it's still not much of a forest until you get over into Missouri."

Finally, Uncle Luther turned onto a narrow lane, drove the buggy up to a two-story, white house, and said, "Whoa, there!" to the horse. Then, over his shoulder, he added, "We're home, Dwight! Tell your aunt Minnie that she needs to wake up!"

Dwight hadn't realized until then that Aunt Minnie had been taking a nap.

"I just had my eyes closed, Luther," Aunt Minnie said. "You know I can't sleep unless I'm lying down."

"Uh-huh," Uncle Luther said. He stepped down and fastened the reins to the front porch railing, then he helped Aunt Minnie and Dwight from the buggy.

Just then, several women dressed similarly to Aunt Minnie came rushing out of the house and headed straight for Dwight. "Hello! Hello! Hello!" they all shouted at once.

Dwight quickly grabbed Aunt Minnie's skirt. He had no idea what was happening. *Why are these women so excited to see me?* he wondered.

It turned out they were all relatives of his mother, and they were very happy that one of her sons had come for a visit. Each one of the women gave Dwight a big hug. With Aunt Minnie and Uncle Luther behind them, the ladies, their full dresses billowing, led him in a whirlwind into the house. There he discovered that not only were there more women like them, but there were also a lot of men. What Dwight didn't see were children his own age. "Where are the children?" Dwight asked.

"Some of them are in school, some of them are sick, and some of them are working in the fields," came the replies.

Suddenly, Dwight wasn't so happy that he had been the only one chosen to come to Topeka with Aunt Minnie. Now, he wished that Arthur and Edgar had also come along with him. At least he would have had somebody to play with.

Finally, the grown-ups all started talking among themselves, and Dwight slipped out the front door without anyone noticing that he had gone.

For several minutes he sat in the front porch swing and let it rock him gently. Even though all of these people were his family, he felt lonesome and lost among them. The horse and buggy was still tied to the porch railing, and what Dwight wanted to do more than anything else right then was untie the reins, take the buggy back to Topeka, and then ride the train home to Abilene. The problem was, he didn't know how to do any of those things.

Just then, Uncle Luther came outside and sat down in the swing beside Dwight. "You look like you might be unhappy about something, Dwight," he said.

"No sir, I'm not," Dwight said. "I'm really glad to be here."

Uncle Luther grinned. "Well, I'll tell you one thing," he said. "That sister-in-law of mine has taught her boys to be polite, even if they're not telling the truth."

"But I am telling the—," Dwight started to say, but Uncle Luther stopped him. "I'm on my way to the barn to do the evening chores.

Why don't you come with me so I can show you our new kittens?"

Suddenly, the thought of being able to play with new kittens made Dwight's homesickness almost disappear. "I'd like that very much, Uncle Luther!" he said.

Dwight jumped off the swing and started following Uncle Luther around the house and toward the barn, but they hadn't gone very far down a well-trodden path before two geese came out of some tall grass to their left.

"Oh, they're beautiful!" Dwight said. He looked up at his Uncle Luther. "Can I play with them first?" he asked.

Uncle Luther raised an eyebrow. "Well, you can *try*, if you want, but I need to go on to the barn," he said. "The female goose there, the one in front, is Betsy, and the gander behind her is George, her husband."

"Hi, Betsy," Dwight said.

Uncle Luther chuckled. "You stay here and talk to the geese, and I'll go take care of my chores," he said. "Come on to the barn when you're ready to see the kittens."

"All right, Uncle Luther," Dwight said.

As Uncle Luther headed toward the barn, Dwight and Betsy stood and looked at each other for several moments. Finally, Dwight knelt down on the path and said, "Here, Betsy! Here, goosey, goosey! Come let me pet you!"

But Betsy remained where she was, just looking at Dwight, not moving an inch. Dwight stood up and started toward her.

Suddenly, Dwight heard a strange hissing noise, unlike anything he'd ever heard before. At that moment, George spread his wings and took a couple of leaps toward Dwight, all the while continuing to hiss.

"Ahhhh!" Dwight cried, jumping back, then turning and running a safe distance away in the direction of Uncle Luther's house.

When Dwight realized that George wasn't following him, he stopped and turned around. George had lowered his wings and was now strutting around Betsy. She still hadn't moved from where she had been standing.

"Well, I don't have to play with you two," Dwight said. "I'll go to the barn and play with the new kittens."

Dwight started toward the barn. He had planned to make a wide circle around George and Betsy, who were still blocking the path. But before Dwight could do that, George once again spread his wings and let out a loud hissing sound. This time, though, George didn't just leap a couple of times in Dwight's direction. He lunged at him and even managed to pinch Dwight's cheek with his bill.

"Oooooh!" Dwight cried, grabbing the side of his face. He couldn't believe how much it hurt. Even though he wanted to, he knew he wouldn't be able to stop the tears.

Quickly, Dwight ran toward the house. When he reached the back door, he jerked it

open and ran inside. Aunt Minnie immediately had her arms open to receive him on her lap.

"Oh, my goodness, Dwight," Aunt Minnie said. "What's wrong?"

Dwight told her.

Just then, the kitchen door opened and Uncle Luther was standing there. Dwight looked up at him. Uncle Luther was holding an old broom in his hands.

"You wouldn't believe what just happened to me," Uncle Luther said. "I was walking back to the house and that silly gander tried to attack me!"

Dwight sat up. "That happened to me, too!" he said.

"Well, he won't try to do that anymore," Uncle Luther said. He held out the broom to Dwight. "I just waved it around and that frightened him off without hurting him."

"Do you think it would work for me, too, Uncle Luther?" Dwight asked.

"Well, I don't know," Uncle Luther said. "I guess you'll just have to try it if you want to see those kittens."

"I do. I do. I really do," Dwight said.

Dwight left the kitchen and started toward the barn. George was strutting around Betsy, who still hadn't moved. When Dwight got close to them, George once again spread his wings and starting making his hissing sound, but this time Dwight held out the broom in front of him and starting thrusting it toward George, saying, "Get out of here! Get out of here!"

George kept flapping his wings and hissing, but he wasn't moving from where he was.

Dwight kept advancing, thrusting the broom at George.

Just when Dwight was almost upon George and Betsy, George gave a loud squawk. Dwight made a final thrust, this time letting some of the broom straws graze George's wings.

Now, Betsy gave a loud squawk, too, and started running back into the tall grass. When George saw her, he followed.

Dwight chased both of them for a few minutes, hollering and laughing triumphantly.

Finally, when he thought that the two geese had been taught a lesson, he went back to the path and continued on to the barn to see the kittens.

Later, when all of the relatives were gone, leaving Dwight alone with Uncle Luther and Aunt Minnie, Uncle Luther said, "Did you learn anything important today, Dwight?"

"Yes sir, I did," Dwight said. "You should always be stronger than your enemy."

School Days

After Dwight got back to Abilene from Topeka, his parents allowed him only one day to be the center of attention. After that, he was expected to return to the family's regular routine.

"I don't want to get up now," Dwight said sleepily on the second morning he was back, after Edgar had told him it was time for breakfast. "Aunt Minnie and Uncle Luther let me stay in bed as long as I wanted to."

"Well, you're home now, Dwight," Edgar said. "You're not on vacation anymore, so get up."

Dwight gave Edgar a steely stare and turned over to face the wall.

Behind him, Dwight heard Edgar charging the bed. Within seconds, Edgar was on top of him and pommeling his face, but Dwight had expected it and had positioned himself so he could burrow under Edgar's body. He was soon on top of him.

"I'll teach you to tell me what to do!" Dwight shouted. "That's not going to happen anymore!"

Now, it was his turn to pummel Edgar, but that lasted for only a few seconds before Edgar was once again on top. For the next few minutes they took turns pounding each other until a voice from the door said, "Stop that fighting!"

Dwight recognized his mother's stern voice, but although Edgar stopped instantly, Dwight managed to get in one last punch, which flung Edgar off his bed and onto the floor.

"Stand up, both of you," Mrs. Eisenhower commanded.

Dwight knew better than to disobey his mother much longer. He jumped off the bed, but he didn't help Edgar, who was struggling to get up off the floor.

"Dwight, I want you to get dressed and come to the parlor right now. You have responsibilities in this family, and I expect you to take care of them," Mrs. Eisenhower said. She turned to Edgar. "I don't remember telling you to have a fight with your brother." As she turned to leave, she added, "We'll be waiting for you both to join us for Bible study."

Dwight knew that if he didn't hurry, he'd be in even more trouble, so he ignored Edgar's taunts and got dressed.

When Edgar finally realized that Dwight wasn't going to take his bait, he left the room. Edgar was already sitting in the parlor with the rest of the family, a smirk on his face, when Dwight finally got there.

Dwight took his seat, aware that it was so quiet, you could hear a pin drop.

Mrs. Eisenhower started reading the first chapter of Genesis, and Dwight realized that the family had finished Revelations while he was in Topeka, and was starting over. He was disappointed that he had missed what he thought was the scariest book of the Bible. He had heard it all before, but he never got tired of listening to his mother read to them.

When Mrs. Eisenhower reached the seventh verse of Genesis, Chapter 1, she stopped and handed the Bible to Edgar.

Dwight and Edgar eyed each other. Without even saying anything, Dwight was sure Edgar knew what he was thinking. It was a privilege in the Eisenhower family to be allowed to read the Bible, but that privilege was taken away if you made a mistake. Much to Dwight's disappointment, Edgar read the next three chapters without making one error. When Edgar handed the Bible back to his mother, he smirked at Dwight again. It was all Dwight could do to keep from lunging at his brother from across the room.

After breakfast, the entire family set about cleaning the house and making it ready for the arrival of the other members of a new religious group that the Eisenhower family now belonged to. They called themselves the Bible Students. At each meeting, they would sing songs, with Mrs. Eisenhower playing the piano, and share what the Scripture lessons meant to them.

Dwight was glad that he and his brothers weren't expected to sit through the long meetings. However, even outside, while he and the children of the other Bible Students were playing blindman's bluff and hide-and-seek, Dwight couldn't help hearing part of the services. Often, after he was in bed and his other brothers were asleep, what he had heard during the day would play over and over in his mind. As he slowly drifted toward sleep, he would hear his mother saying, "We should all ask for God's guidance in making the right decisions."

In September 1896, when Dwight was almost six, he started school at Lincoln Elementary, which was near his house on the south side of Abilene. For the next three years he spent most of the school year, from September to June, trying to figure out why it was necessary for him to be there.

Unlike the elementary school in the north part of the town, Lincoln had no lights or indoor plumbing. Also, during the winter months, when the cold north wind raked across Abilene, the place was dark and scary.

One snowy morning in early November, as was his usual custom, Mr. Eisenhower stood at the bottom of the stairs at 5:30 A.M. and called, "Boys! It's time to get up!"

Dwight groaned. He had awakened with a stomachache and decided that he wasn't going to school that day.

Sending Edgar on ahead, Mrs. Eisenhower listened to Dwight's reason.

"I'm not going because I'll have to spend most of the day in that freezing outhouse," Dwight told her. "Why did they have to build the toilets on the north side of the school, anyway?"

"Well, I still think that . . ." Mrs. Eisenhower hesitated.

Dwight thought she seemed at a loss for words, so he added, "Anyway, Mama, school's no place for boys. Our teacher always pays more attention to the girls. The other boys and I just sit there, repeating over and over what she says, which doesn't amount to a hill of beans."

Mrs. Eisenhower let out a big sigh. "Dwight, why do you always . . ."

Once again, Mrs. Eisenhower stopped, but this time it was because Alfred Brenner had stuck his head through the partially open door of the bedroom and said, "Edgar told me you weren't coming to school today, Dwight! You have to. We're going to play shinny at recess."

"Really?" Dwight said.

The game, much like ice hockey, but played with long sticks and a tin can, was one of Dwight's favorites.

Alfred nodded. "You need to be there, too, or we won't have a chance of winning," he said.

"I'll meet you out front in two minutes," Dwight said. He jumped into his pants and finished buttoning his shirt. "I'm feeling better, Mama," he called as he raced out of the room and out of the house.

Alfred gave Dwight one of the two perfectly proportioned sticks he had been holding. "My father made these for us," he said. "I told him that mine was no good and that you broke yours during the last game."

"Thanks, Al," Dwight said. "We can win all of our games with these."

Alfred held up a new tin can. "Mother also gave me this," he said. "With our new clubs, we'll be able to get this puck in the goal every time we hit it."

The tardy bell had already sounded when Dwight and Alfred got to school, but the principal had a couple of the fifth graders by the ears, so he ignored Dwight and Alfred. They slipped into their class before the teacher realized they were late.

At first, Dwight's mind was only on the upcoming game of shinny, but when his teacher announced that they were going to have a spelling bee, he momentarily forgot about it. There were very few things in school that could interest him, but winning a spelling bee was one of them.

Unfortunately, just as Dwight had predicted to his mother, he ended up spending most of the day in the freezing outhouse and could not participate in either the spelling bee or the shinny game.

• • •

Dwight also liked arithmetic. His math skills, along with his ability to spell better than most of his classmates, usually helped keep him out of trouble with his teachers in subjects he didn't excel in. Penmanship was the exception.

"Oh, my goodness, Dwight!" Mrs. Stein exclaimed one day in class. "I see you stopped by the chicken pen before you came to class."

Several of the girls giggled, but Dwight looked up at his teacher with a puzzled expression. "No, ma'am, I didn't," he said.

Mrs. Stein rained an eyebrow. "Well, how do you explain the chicken scratches on your paper, then?" she asked.

Dwight blushed.

Now, the boys in the class were also laughing.

"I'm just teasing you, Dwight," Mrs. Stein said. "If I can't read what you've written, then how can I give you a grade for it?"

"I try, Mrs. Stein, but my hands just weren't

made for this fancy writing," Dwight said. He held them up for Mrs. Stein to see. "These hands were made to hold an ax, so they can chop wood for the stove, or even a hunting rifle, so they can put game on the table."

Mrs. Stein cleared her throat. "Well, if you don't do something about your penmanship, Dwight David Eisenhower," she said huffily, "then you'll never, ever amount to anything in this life."

That evening after supper, while Dwight, Edgar, and Arthur were washing the dishes, Dwight told his brothers everything that Mrs. Stein had said.

"She doesn't know what she's talking about," Arthur said. "You know how to do lots of things at school that don't require your being able to write well."

"Like what?" Dwight said sullenly.

"You're good at sports, especially baseball," Edgar said. "Here! Catch!" He threw one of the plates he had been drying to Dwight.

Dwight caught it one-handed and grinned. "You're right," he said.

Arthur pretended to run to home plate. "The runner's heading home, Dwight!" he shouted. "Throw it!"

Dwight threw the plate to Arthur, who caught it and pretended to tag the runner.

"He's out!" Edgar shouted.

"See? What'd we tell you, Dwight? You're good!" Arthur said as he handed Dwight the plate to be rewashed. "If you've never once dropped one of Mama's plates, then why would you ever drop a baseball?"

Dwight knew his brothers were right about his athletic skills. If there was only a way he could turn sports into some way to earn a living, then he wouldn't have to worry about pleasing Mrs. Stein, and he might even quit school.

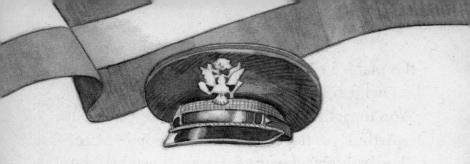

Playing War

On January 25, 1898, the twenty-four-gun United States battleship *Maine* dropped anchor in Havana harbor on the Spanish-controlled island of Cuba. Although for many months there had been talk of war between the United States and Spain, everyone was told that the *Maine* was just paying the island a friendly visit. Actually, the *Maine* had been sent to Cuba by President William McKinley to protect Americans and American property on the island. But tensions between the United States and Spain soon increased, and on the evening of February 15, the *Maine* erupted in an enormous explosion, killing 266 crew members. Spain was blamed. On April 25, the United States Congress declared that America was at war with Spain. Over the next few months, the United States defeated the Spanish in several battles. However, the one that captured the imagination of most Americans was the Cuban Battle of San Juan Hill, in which Colonel Teddy Roosevelt's Rough Riders forced the Spaniards to flee from the city of Santiago de Cuba.

At the breakfast table one Saturday morning in August, Mr. Eisenhower mentioned that the United States had signed a peace treaty with Spain. There was talk that Cuba would be free and that the United States would take over possession of the Philippines, Guam, and Puerto Rico. Eight-year-old Dwight's eyes lit up. He turned to his brothers and said, "I know what we're going to play today."

"Remember the *Maine*!" Edgar shouted.

Dwight nodded.

Ever since the explosion in Havana harbor in February, which started the Spanish-American War, the Eisenhower boys had been thoroughly fascinated by the events that had followed. Whenever they got the chance, they rounded up a group of friends to reenact the different battles, especially the Battle of San Juan Hill.

After being dismissed from the breakfast table, the boys all headed outside.

"Do you think we can get the carnival kids to be the Spaniards again?" Edgar said.

"I think so," Dwight told him. "It doesn't seem to bother them to be the enemy."

Some of the boys whose families worked for the carnival often had to fend for themselves while their parents were out of town. They were more than happy to be involved in something other than their jobs of keeping the extra carnival equipment in good repair.

With Dwight in the lead and Arthur, Edgar, and Roy behind him, they headed out into the neighborhood to gather their "troops" for battle. Mostly, they only had to walk down the center of the dirt street before the troops started pouring out of the houses along the way. This was just like how men had joined the army during the Revolutionary War and the Civil War, Dwight told everyone.

Finally, they had enough American troops and, with the carnival boys having agreed once again to be the Spanish troops, the soldiers all headed toward a tiny knoll that served as San Juan Hill.

"I'm Teddy Roosevelt!" Dwight shouted, raising a wooden sword that he continually brandished as he charged up and down "San Juan Hill."

After several charges up the knoll, Edgar grabbed Dwight's arm and shouted, "I'm tougher than you are. Why can't I be Teddy Roosevelt?"

Dwight was sure that if the "Spanish troops" hadn't heard Edgar's request, he might have let his brother be Roosevelt just this once, but there was no way Dwight was going to look weak in front of the "enemy."

"Do you really think so?" Dwight challenged him. "Well, I guess we'll just have to decide this right now."

Dwight threw down his wooden sword and charged Edgar. Edgar fell to the ground with a thud, but managed to roll Dwight over and was soon on top of him. Edgar was only able to land a couple of punches on Dwight's face, though, before Dwight turned the tables. Soon, they were rolling down the knoll, to the laughter of not only the Spanish troops but the American troops as well.

Noses bloody, mouths full of dirt, Edgar and Dwight stood up and had to face finger-pointing from both sides of the war. The soldiers seemed to have forgotten that they were enemies.

"If you don't stop laughing, I'll take you all on!" Dwight shouted at them.

"And I'll help him," Edgar added.

The laughter stopped. Everyone knew that the Eisenhower brothers might fight among themselves, but they also fought for one another when it was necessary.

Dwight picked up his sword and started toward home. Edgar was right behind him, followed by Arthur and Roy.

When Mrs. Eisenhower saw them, she didn't say anything but went immediately to a cabinet in the kitchen where she kept all of the home remedies she needed for what was a never-ending succession of injuries that seemed to befall her sons.

After Dwight and Edgar had washed off the dirt and the blood, Mrs. Eisenhower opened a large glass jar, dipped in a tablespoon, and said, "Open up, boys, it's time for molasses and sulfur."

"No, Mama!" Edgar pleaded.

"That tastes awful," Dwight added.

"Of course it does, but if you liked it, it wouldn't be good for you. Everybody knows that," Mrs. Eisenhower said. "And I firmly believe that molasses and sulfur will take care of anything you shouldn't have inside you and scare off anything that's thinking about paying you a visit."

Dutifully, both boys opened their mouths because they knew there was no escaping their mother's remedies.

Before Mrs. Eisenhower allowed them to leave, though, she said, "Sit down. I want to talk to you about something."

Dwight looked at Edgar. He was trying to remember if he had done something he had forgotten about but for which he was now going to be punished.

"I don't want you playing that game anymore," Mrs. Eisenhower told them. "War is wicked. It's a sin. It's not anything that you should have fun with."

Dwight looked over at Edgar and gave him a knowing grin. They both were thinking the same thing: If playing war was something you shouldn't do because it was a sin, then that made it all the more appealing.

Later that afternoon, as Dwight and Edgar were hoeing weeds in the garden, Dwight saw his mother filling up the large metal tub with water that had been heated in a barrel in the backyard. Since all of the boys had to use this one tub for their baths, without a change of water, Dwight always tried to be first so he wouldn't have to wash off in his brothers' dirty bath water. Since he wasn't usually successful, he avoided taking a bath as much as he could. But today he was hot and sticky, not only from doing his chores but from playing war all morning. He also couldn't stand the way he smelled.

"I've got a headache, Edgar. I'm going to go lie down," Dwight said. "I'll finish hoeing later."

Dwight put away his hoe, then hurried to the house, holding his head and moaning slightly. Once he was inside, he ran upstairs, undressed as quickly and as quietly as he could, then he tiptoed downstairs, naked, but holding a set of clean clothes in his hand.

When Dwight reached the bottom of the stairs, he listened carefully. When the coast was clear, he made a dash for the kitchen door, ready to jump into the tub. However, Dwight screeched to a halt when he saw Edgar already sitting in it.

"You thought I didn't know what you were doing, did you, Dwight, telling me that you had a headache and were going to lie down?" Edgar said, taunting him. He raised his left arm and made a big production of soaping his armpits. "I know all of your tricks."

Dwight gritted his teeth. Sometimes Edgar made him so angry, he couldn't stand it. For some reason, Edgar always seemed to find ways to outsmart him. Of all of his brothers, Edgar was the one he wish lived somewhere else.

"I sure was dirty, Dwight," Edgar continued. He looked down at the water. "You can't even see the bottom of the tub, this water is so dirty."

Dwight whirled around and ran back upstairs. He knew of a nearby pond that had cleaner water than the tub, so he quickly redressed, then grabbed a chunk of soap on his way out of the kitchen.

"Where are you going?" Edgar shouted to him.

Dwight didn't answer. Outside, he jumped on his father's solid-tire bicycle and headed south of town.

That night at supper, Dwight sat on his usual stool and waited for his father to finish grace. He knew that the subject of the bath would come up, and he was well prepared. When Mr. Eisenhower had finished and had started passing the serving dishes around, Edgar said, "Why didn't you take a bath today, Dwight?"

Without missing a beat, Dwight said, "I did, Edgar," and helped himself to some English peas.

"No, you didn't," Edgar said.

"Yes, I did," Dwight insisted.

"No, you—," Edgar started to repeat, but Mrs. Eisenhower stopped the argument with, "Did you take a bath today, Dwight?"

"Yes, ma'am," Dwight said. He stood up and walked around the other side of the table to where his mother was sitting. "Smell me."

"Dwight, please," Mrs. Eisenhower said.

"Nobody believes me, so I want to prove it," Dwight insisted. "Smell me."

Mrs. Eisenhower first sniffed Dwight's skin and then his clothes. "Well, I guess you did, after all," she announced. She turned to Edgar. "The subject of your brother's bath is closed, so please finish your supper."

"Yes, ma'am," Edgar said.

For the rest of the meal, Mr. Eisenhower answered Mrs. Eisenhower's questions about what had taken place that day at the creamery, but usually only with one-syllable words. He preferred instead to concentrate on the food in front of him. Mrs. Eisenhower talked about some of the things she had asked God to help her understand.

Finally, Mrs. Eisenhower said, "Amen!" which was the signal that everyone was now permitted to leave the table.

Dwight got up immediately because he knew that Edgar would try to beat out of him where he had taken a bath, and he wasn't about to let anyone else in on that secret.

The New House

In the summer of 1898, when Dwight was almost eight, his Uncle Abe decided that he was going to leave Abilene. Although Abe was Dwight's favorite uncle and Dwight was going to miss him, he was excited that his family would get to move into his uncle's house, which was two blocks from where they now lived.

"Why are you leaving Abilene, Uncle Abe?" Dwight asked him one night at the supper table.

"I've got an itchy foot, Dwight," his uncle

told him. "Your aunt Ara and I want to take the 'gospel wagon' out to the western part of the state and maybe even down into Oklahoma Territory."

Dwight knew all about Uncle Luther's "gospel wagon." It had once been used to haul bales of hay, which were sold to farmers around Abilene to feed their cattle, but now it was part church, part house. A pulpit had been built at the rear of the wagon from which Uncle Luther could preach his sermons. The rest of it was covered by a canvas tarp, and that was where his uncle and aunt would live during their travels.

"We plan to show people the way to heaven," his aunt Ara added. "We've been commanded to do so by the good Lord and can no longer ignore him."

Dwight looked over at Arthur, who had raised his eyebrows. He loved his uncle, although Dwight had never really understood him. Dwight did know, however, that

Uncle Abe could raise an audience out of the dust with his sermons.

"Well, good luck to you, Uncle Abe," Dwight said.

The two-story white frame house at 201 Southeast Fourth Street was surrounded by large maple trees and sat on three acres of land that included a large barn. Dwight was a little disappointed after his family finally moved in, though. They didn't seem to have as much room as he had thought they would.

"What happened?" Dwight asked Arthur one evening.

"Earl Dewey happened, that's what," Edgar answered for him.

With the addition of baby Earl just a few months before, the Eisenhower family now numbered seven, and the house that Dwight remembered in his head as being very spacious barely gave him any more room to breathe.

"This house seemed so much larger when Uncle Abe lived here," Dwight complained to his mother. "It's still hard to get anything done."

"Once we get organized again, Dwight," Mrs. Eisenhower told him, "you won't feel that way, I can assure you, *if you cooperate.*"

"Yes, ma'am," Dwight said.

His mother was right, Dwight soon realized. It wasn't long before the new house and the land it sat on became all things to the family: football field, chapel, boxing arena, emergency hospital, study hall, and cooking school.

One morning, just a few weeks after they had moved into their new house, Mrs. Eisenhower, holding Earl in her arms, called all the boys into the kitchen.

"I have written down a list of your new chores, and after I read them out to you, I'm going to tack the list to the cupboard," Mrs. Eisenhower said, "in case you should forget what you're supposed to be doing."

Inwardly, Dwight groaned. He knew that every household in Abilene had chores that had to be done daily, but most of the other families had *girls* to do them.

Why did I have to have so many brothers? Dwight asked himself. *Why couldn't I have had some sisters who could do all these things that girls are supposed to do?*

Mrs. Eisenhower began reading the list, which had the names of the chores and the dates and times each one of the boys was supposed to do them. The chores included not only outside work but also inside work, such as washing the dishes, doing the laundry, and even cooking the meals.

"Are there any questions, boys?" Mrs. Eisenhower asked.

There were none.

"Good," Mrs. Eisenhower said, shifting Earl to her other arm. "This morning you are all going to plant the seeds your father bought at the grain store yesterday. You'll plant them in the plots of land assigned to each one of you to use for a garden."

Dwight was glad that they could spend some time outside, before any of the inside chores started. He actually liked the idea of having a garden, because that way he could grow what he wanted to eat. But there was an added bonus. Their mother told them that they could keep any money they made from selling their vegetables. Dwight's thoughts turned immediately from worrying about what food to grow for meals to buying new baseballs and mitts. It hadn't taken him long to realize that he didn't mind eating whatever vegetables his mother put in front of him if it meant he'd be able to use his own money for new equipment for all the sports he loved to play.

Later, as everyone was getting ready for bed, Arthur said, "When Billy Schmidt found out that I cooked, he told me he was jealous."

Dwight wrinkled his nose. "Why?" he asked.

"He said his mother and his sisters are terrible cooks, but they won't let him or his older brother or his father in the kitchen."

"Are you serious?" Dwight said.

"Yes, I'm serious," Arthur said. "Billy said he'd give anything if he could cook for himself, because that way he wouldn't be so hungry all the time."

Dwight thought about that for several minutes after the lights were out. Finally, right before he fell asleep, he decided that knowing how to cook and to wash dishes and to do laundry might not be such a bad thing after all. He was certainly learning to take care of himself.

Some chores, though, Dwight quickly decided, were not worth his time. Collecting kindling for the stove and shaving it into pieces was one of them, but there was no excuse he could think of to keep from having to do it.

Finally, one morning, Dwight thought he had figured out a possible solution to the problem. Earl had started crying after Mrs. Eisenhower had told Dwight that the wood box next to the stove was almost empty and that he needed to collect some wood, shave it, and fill up the box. Mrs. Eisenhower picked up Earl and began humming to him softly, and Earl quit crying.

"Thank you, Mama," Edgar said as he passed by and headed up to the second floor to sweep. "That was getting on my nerves."

"I know, dear," Mrs. Eisenhower said. "It was getting on mine, too."

Suddenly, Dwight knew how he could get out of doing chores that he detested.

He waited until his mother had told him two more times to go collect the kindling. Then he picked up the wood box, but as he started slowly toward the back door, he began crying as loud as he could, trying to sound as though something really awful had just happened to him.

Dwight was absolutely amazed at how easily the tears poured out of his eyes and down his cheeks. He was sure his mother was going to treat him just like she had baby Earl. She would pat him on the back, hum to him softly, and then tell him that he didn't have to go gather the kindling if he didn't want to.

When he was almost to the back door, though, Mrs. Eisenhower not only had said nothing to him but she hadn't even seemed to notice what he was doing. She had put Earl down on a pallet and was now peeling potatoes and putting them in a large pot.

Finally, Dwight reached the back door and touched the knob. *I'll give her one more chance to stop me,* he decided and, with that, he let out a bloodcurdling scream that turned into exaggerated sobs. Still, Mrs. Eisenhower continued to peel the potatoes. Only baby

Earl was staring at him, Dwight could see out of the corner of one eye.

Now, Dwight was angry. He pulled open the back door and hurried out into the yard, bawling at the top of his lungs. He cried all of the way to the pile of kindling. He cried while he was shaving the wood. He cried while he was putting the shavings into the box. He cried as he headed back toward the back door, but halfway there, his tears cleared up enough that he could see one of their neighbors, Mrs. Laak, standing at the door, pounding on it, shouting, "Mrs. Eisenhower! Mrs. Eisenhower!"

Dwight stopped crying, but kept sniffing, and hurried to see what was wrong.

Just as he got to the back door, it opened, and Mrs. Eisenhower was standing there, a large smile on her face. "Good morning to you, Mrs. Laak," Mrs. Eisenhower said politely. "How are you today?"

"Well, I'm fine, Mrs. Eisenhower, but . . . ,"

Mrs. Laak said, turning to look at Dwight, "what have you been doing to your son here to cause him so much pain?"

"Oh, he'll be all right, Mrs. Laak, just as soon as he brings the kindling in, I promise you," Mrs. Eisenhower said, the smile never leaving her face. "There are some chores that our Dwight doesn't particularly like to do."

Dwight could feel his face turning bright red. "Excuse me, please," he said as he walked between his mother and Mrs. Laak and set the wood box next to the stove. Without turning around, Dwight called over his shoulder, "I'm going over to Bob's house, Mama! I'll be back in time for supper."

"All right, dear," Mrs. Eisenhower called back sweetly.

It was all Dwight could do to control his anger before he reached the front door. Once he was outside, out of shouting distance of his house, he let out a yell that released all of his frustrations. He loved his parents dearly, but sometimes they exasperated him in ways he couldn't explain. There was never any reasoning with them. His father and mother knew exactly what they wanted for themselves and for their sons, and there was no changing their minds.

As Dwight headed down the street toward Bob Davis's house, he wished that the man were his father—a thought he had had several times recently. Dwight felt guilty about that, so much so that he tried to keep it from coming into his head, but he was seldom successful.

It seemed to Dwight that Bob Davis knew how to do everything. He made his living as a fisherman, a guide, and a trapper. Dwight had only known Bob for a few weeks, but in that short amount of time, they had gone fishing, trapping, duck hunting, cooked over a campfire, and had even poled a flatboat with a single pole down the Solomon River.

Today, though, when Dwight knocked on

Bob's front door, he was greeted with, "When you leave here, son, you're going to be the best poker player in Kansas—next to me, of course."

For the rest of the afternoon, Bob taught Dwight how to play the card game, which was based on percentages and odds. Since Dwight was already good at mathematics, it wasn't long before he was starting to outplay Bob.

"Well, it's getting late, Dwight," Bob said. "I think we need to quit."

"Ah, you're just saying that because I'm beating you," Dwight teased him. "Why don't we play another hand?"

Bob shook his head. "There's a lesson here, too, Dwight," he said.

"What's that?" Dwight asked.

"No matter how good you are at this game, you should always know when to quit, and that's what I know now." He grinned. "If you work at it, son, one of these days you might earn a few extra bucks at the poker table, and that could help you buy some things you might not otherwise be able to afford."

Dwight grinned. "I'll remember that," he said.

When he got home that evening, he was full of swagger and, seeing Earl crawling around on the floor, he announced, "Come with me out to the toolshed, Earl. I'm going to make you a toy."

"Well, I'm certainly glad to see that you're in such a good mood," Mrs. Eisenhower said.

Dwight smiled at her and scooped up Earl in his arms.

"Make sure you watch him carefully, Dwight," Mrs. Eisenhower called to him as they headed out the back door. "Don't let him get into anything."

When Dwight and Earl got to the tool-shed, Dwight spread an old quilt down on the floor for Earl to play on. "Now, you just stay there and watch, and when I'm finished, you'll have a new toy to play with."

Dwight, still thinking about how good he now was at poker and about the possibilities of winning a lot of money one of these days, picked up a couple of knives off the work-table. He laid them on a windowsill, and then looked around for some pieces of wood he could carve into a dog, an animal that Earl seemed especially to like. He had just found what he thought would be perfect, when Earl let out a tiny scream.

Dwight turned around and saw to his horror that Earl had evidently climbed up on the chair, grabbed one of the knives from the windowsill, and then fallen off the chair. The knife had struck him in the left eye.

For Dwight, the next several hours were a blur. Earl was taken to the hospital, where the family learned that the eye was permanently damaged.

When they were all finally back home, Mr. and Mrs. Eisenhower gathered everyone in the parlor.

"Life is always going to be full of risks, boys, and accidents will happen, but nothing good ever came from keeping anger bottled up inside you," Mrs. Eisenhower said. "So I don't want anybody in this family ever blaming Dwight for what happened to Earl."

But Dwight knew that for the rest of his life he would know that what had happened to his brother really was all his fault. That night, he cried himself to sleep.

Life with Five Brothers

By the spring of 1900, nine-year-old Dwight
could hardly remember ever having lived in
the house on Second Street. Their new house
sat on plenty of land, and there was room to
mark off a baseball diamond. Now Dwight
and his brothers could play what he thought
of as his true love. With Milton's birth the
previous September, Dwight told everyone
that it wouldn't be long before they could
field a complete team!

"One of these days, I'm going to be a short-
stop just like Honus Wagner," Dwight told

Bob Davis one evening as they sat around a campfire, after a full day of fishing in Mud Creek. "I might even play for the Pittsburgh Pirates, too."

"Well, I've seen you play several times, Dwight, and you're more than just good, you're professional, and I'm telling you the truth about that," Bob said. "I've been to several of those professional baseball games before, and I've got a good eye for picking out boys who've got a future in the game, and I think you'd be one of the best."

Dwight sat up. "Do you really, Bob?" he asked excitedly. "Why haven't you ever told me that before?"

"Well, I never knew you were interested in playing baseball for a living, Dwight," Bob replied. "After all, you're good at so many things, you can just take your pick."

Dwight grinned. "You're the only person who ever tells me that, Bob, so I don't really know it until I hear it from you," he said. "My parents love me, there's no doubt about that, but they won't hold to any arrogance, so none of us boys goes around talking about how good he is. Well, at least not in front of Mama and Papa."

"My old man was the same way, Dwight," Bob said. He let out a long sigh. "I don't remember my mama. She died when I was still pretty young, but from all the pictures I've seen of her, I don't think she would have been that way. I think she would have told me if I was good at something."

Dwight stretched, then said, "Ouch!"

"What's the matter?" Bob asked.

"I got sunburned when I went swimming," he said. "I hope it doesn't still hurt tomorrow, because we've got a big game coming up and, well, who knows, there might be a scout from the Pittsburgh Pirates there to watch me play."

Bob nodded. "You never can tell, Dwight," he said, "but they never let anybody know they're there, so you should always play as if your whole life depended on it."

"I always do, Bob," Dwight said. "I always do!"

Just as Dwight arrived home the next morning from the camping trip, he heard a loud yell coming from the kitchen.

He raced into the room to see what the matter was. There was a bloody tooth hanging from a string attached to a doorknob.

Seven-year-old Roy was holding the side of his jaw. "That hurt, Mama," he managed to say.

Mrs. Eisenhower handed him a white cloth that had been folded up in little squares. "Sit down in that chair over there, Roy," she said, "and bite down on this cloth until the medicine I put on it starts to work."

Dwight shuddered at the thought of a string tied to one of his teeth. Most of the time, when he was younger and his teeth needed to come out, he tried to pull them out himself, in order to save himself from the string tied to the door.

"Dwight, you're just in time to clean out the chicken coop," Mrs. Eisenhower said.

"Aw, Mama, do I have to?" Dwight said. "I'm tired from camping."

Mrs. Eisenhower turned and gave him a hard look. "Now, Dwight David Eisenhower, do you think I'd be wasting my breath telling you to do something that I didn't think really needed to be done?" she asked.

Dwight shook his head. "No, ma'am," he replied.

"I'll do it for you, Mama," Edgar said as he came into the kitchen. "I don't mind that at all." He headed toward the back door. "See you later, Dwight."

Dwight watched his brother disappear and wondered what in the world he was up to. It only took him a couple of minutes to find out.

"Well, I guess since Edgar is going to do

that chore, then you'll have to do the only one left," Mrs. Eisenhower said. "You'd better start boiling the water for the machine, because Earl's and Milton's diapers need to be washed."

Dwight gritted his teeth. *Edgar knew all along that if I cleaned out the chicken coop, he'd be stuck with our brothers' smelly diapers,* he thought. *He outsmarted me this time, but I'll get him back some way.*

Dwight knew it wouldn't do him any good to complain about this chore, so he set about pumping water. He poured it into a big kettle just outside the back door, which the family used to heat large amounts of water. Finally, there was enough to fill the washing machine. Dwight put all of Earl's and Milton's soiled diapers into the scalding water and started churning them up and down with a sawed-off broom handle until they began to get clean.

"I sure will be glad when Earl and Milton

stop messing in their diapers," Dwight muttered. "I may train them to use the chamber pot myself!"

"Good luck," Edgar said.

Dwight turned around, dipped his hand down in the soapy water, and came up with a handful of suds. He slung it at his brother, but Edgar ducked, and the soap suds hit the wall and dribbled down it to a soapy puddle. Dwight had to listen to Edgar laughing as he ran upstairs to their room.

Mrs. Eisenhower chose to come into the room at the same time, and she didn't think there was anything funny about soapsuds on the wall, so she said, "When you've finished, I want you to push Earl around the yard in his baby buggy."

"All right, Mama," Dwight agreed.

Out of the corner of one eye, Dwight saw his mother give him a suspicious look. He knew it was because he was suddenly so agreeable about doing a task that she thought he found boring. But the last time he'd had to push the buggy, Dwight had figured out a way to make it easier.

When Dwight finally finished washing the dirty diapers, he said, "Come on, Earl, it's time to go for a ride."

Dwight knew that Earl always enjoyed the buggy rides, so he didn't have to be coaxed.

Dwight put his brother inside the buggy, then he headed outside. This time, he pushed Earl to the other side of the barn so that no one from the house could see them. When they got there, Dwight laid an old quilt on the grass, put a history book on it, then tied one end of a piece of rope to the buggy's axle and the other end to his foot. For the next hour, he lay on the blanket, reading his book, as he pulled the buggy toward him with his leg, then pushed it back the same way. Earl didn't seem to mind how his brother pushed him in the buggy, as long as it was moving, and Dwight got to read at the same

time that he was supposed to be performing one of his chores.

One Sunday morning, Dwight and Edgar returned home after Sunday school and decided to prepare dinner so it would be ready for the rest of the family when they got back.

After they had finished with the meat, the vegetables, and the bread, Dwight said, "Let's make an apple pie for dessert."

Edgar went to the cellar to bring in a jar of pie apples that his mother had canned the previous autumn. Dwight got out the bowls, the flour, and the lard, and started making the dough for the crust.

When Edgar returned, he set the table; then, just as he finished, Dwight yelled, "Here! Catch!"

Dwight threw the mound of pie dough at his brother, but Edgar missed it. He quickly picked up the dough, brushed off the dirt, and threw it back to Dwight. For the next several minutes, they played catch with the dough, which landed on the floor several times. Finally, they decided it was time to roll it out and bake the shell for the pie.

When the rest of the family returned home, they were pleasantly surprised by the delicious meal that awaited them. Only Arthur remarked that the crust seemed to be a strange color. Nothing more was said about it, although Dwight was sure that his older brother knew it had probably been used in a game of baseball before it had found its way into the oven.

"These are delicious potatoes, boys," Mrs. Eisenhower said. "You did a wonderful job."

"Song!" Earl cried.

Dwight grinned at his little brother. Since potatoes were served at almost every meal the Eisenhowers ate, Dwight had made up a song, which he and his brothers sang with gusto.

"Oh, the 'taters they grew small,
And we ate them skin and all,
    Out in Kansas . . ."

The next afternoon, Dwight spent a couple of hours sitting at the soda fountain in the back of Case's Department Store downtown. He loved to eat the chocolate sundaes they made there. Today, he had decided to splurge on the treat by using some of the money he had made from selling his vegetables in the north part of Abilene.

When Dwight finally had scraped the last of the ice cream and chocolate from the sundae bowl, he walked over to a rack on which there were magazines for sale. He was delighted to find the latest Wild West stories, so he could read about Bat Masterson, Wild Bill Hickok, Jesse James, and Billy the Kid. Dwight decided he had enough money to buy two of the magazines, so he chose carefully and walked up to the counter, where he paid Mr. Case.

"I haven't read those yet, Dwight," Mr. Case said. "If you like them, then I'll buy them back from you or trade you for some new ones."

"All right, Mr. Case," Dwight said.

He probably wouldn't take Mr. Case up on the offer, though, Dwight decided, as he headed toward home. As long as he had money, he'd continue to buy new magazines and keep the older ones, so he could reread them when he wanted to relive the thrilling adventures. Sometimes at night, he lay awake wondering what it would be like to do something really exciting and if people would want to write about all the things that happened to him.

The Toughest Kid in Abilene

In the summer of 1900, Dwight's vegetable garden flourished because of just the right amount of rain, sunshine, and hoeing out the weeds. When the plants and the vines produced their bumper crops of squash, tomatoes, okra, and beans, Dwight was able to sell everything for a lot of money, but only to the people in the north part of Abilene, who could afford to buy such things.

Now that he was almost ten, Dwight had begun to feel the difference between the people who lived in south Abilene and the people who lived in north Abilene. Until then, Dwight had always been able to ignore the rude comments from the children who lived in the north part of town, but as these wealthier boys and girls got older, too, their remarks about the people who lived on the wrong side of the railroad tracks got meaner.

One day, Dwight had just finished selling the last of his vegetables to a Mrs. Lyons, who, even though she lived on the north side of town, was one of the nicest people he had ever met. Unfortunately, she lived next door to the Martin brothers, who seemed determined to force Dwight to fight them.

"Hey, Eisenhower, you're too poor to be in this part of Abilene," Robert Martin shouted as Dwight left Mrs. Lyons's front porch. "What are you doing around here?"

"He's begging money from us rich folks, that's what," John Martin said.

Dwight threw down the empty bushel basket he'd carried the vegetables in and clinched his fists. "I was not begging for money," he shouted at the Martin brothers. "I raised these vegetables myself, and I was selling them to make money to buy what I want, just like every other merchant in Abilene, including your father."

The Martin brothers started laughing and slapping each other on the back.

"What's so funny?" Dwight demanded.

"Our father's a lawyer, not a *merchant*," John said. "He doesn't *sell* anything."

"Your kind isn't welcome around here, Eisenhower," Robert added. "You'd better get out of this neighborhood before we make you."

Dwight knew his parents disapproved of fighting or even quarreling, although they didn't expect him to tolerate being bullied. Dwight wasn't about to let the brothers run him off. He knew that the only place he could really make any money selling his vegetables was in the north part of Abilene.

To Dwight's surprise, the Martin brothers stayed where they were. Usually, the boys in the northern part of Abilene hurried into their house when Dwight stood up to them.

"What are you going to do, Eisenhower?" John shouted at him. "Throw your rotten tomatoes at us?"

Robert laughed at his brother's joke.

"My tomatoes aren't rotten!" Dwight shouted back.

Finally, Dwight had had enough of these two smart alecks. He threw down his basket and started running toward them.

Both Martin boys turned and raced as fast as they could toward the front door of their house and disappeared inside.

Dwight dusted off his hands, went back to the middle of the street, picked up the bushel basket, and started toward the south part of town. He was shaking from the encounter. Dwight kept his head up straight, but he moved his eyes from side to side. He wanted to make sure the Martin brothers hadn't regrouped and were now gathering their friends together to attack him.

When Dwight finally reached downtown, which was more or less considered neutral territory by everyone, he let out a sigh of relief. As he made his way along the store-fronts, he recalled something that Bob Davis had once told him. "To feign domination of others is often just as effective as physical force." In other words, the threat of a fight will sometimes accomplish more than actu-ally having the fight. It was a lesson Dwight didn't think he'd ever forget.

Still, Dwight thought he'd probably better tell his father about the incident when he got home, just in case the Martin brothers' father complained to the owner of the creamery.

As it turned out, though, there was no chance to do that. As was usually the case, Mr. Eisenhower came home just in time to say grace before supper, eat in silence, and take a book into his bedroom to read before he went to sleep.

After Dwight had gone to bed that evening, he thought about the role his father played in his life. His father rarely spoke to any of the boys, Dwight knew, and they were always wondering why their father never smiled.

"I don't mean this unkindly, Dwight," Bob had said to him during a camping trip, "but your father has a heart of darkness that is rarely lit."

"I'm glad I have you, Bob. I have friends whose fathers do for them what you do for me," Dwight had said. "Even when my father is around us, he's not really there. Do you know what I mean?"

"I know exactly what you mean," Bob had told him.

Just thinking about that conversation now, Dwight felt a tear trickle down his cheek, but he quickly wiped it away and scolded himself silently for thinking about it. He knew he was only feeling sorry for himself—and a little jealous, too—because he was sure that the Martin brothers' father probably paid more attention to them than his father did to him. However, the most important lesson Dwight had learned from both of his parents was that he and his brothers must think and act for themselves. He should never feel sorry for himself, he knew, and he was sure that he would probably be better prepared for life than the Martin boys would because of this lesson. How many times had he heard both his parents say, "What really counts in life is one's faith and good old-fashioned hard work."

In September of 1902, things started to change. When Dwight was almost twelve years old, he entered Garfield Junior High School, which was located in the north part of Abilene. Since Garfield was the town's only junior high, the students were a mix of boys and girls from both the north and south sides of Abilene.

Dwight wasn't sure what to expect. On the first day of school, he had decided things had gone pretty well, even though none of the students he knew from the north side of town would speak to him or his friends. The students were civil, but that ended at recess.

Dwight and his friend David Coughlin were standing near the baseball diamond. They were talking about what kind of team they'd have that year, now that the north side kids would be included, when a boy who seemed larger than life pushed Dwight in the back.

"It's too bad you white trash from the south side have to dirty up our part of town," the boy said to him.

David looked at Dwight and said, "We'd better go. I think I heard the bell ring."

"You didn't hear any bell ring," the boy said. "You two are just scared."

"I'm not scared," Dwight told the boy.

"Oh yeah, well, I think I'll just bite your ear off, then," the boy said. He lunged at Dwight, grabbed him around the waist, and pulled him to the ground. Within seconds, Dwight felt sharp teeth tearing into his ear.

"Ouch!" Dwight cried.

Just then, the boy let out an *oomph* sound and released his grip on Dwight. "Who did that?" he demanded.

"Let's get out of here!" David shouted.

"You kicked me in the stomach!" the boy shouted to David. "Now, I'm going to get both of you."

Dwight and David took off running, with the tall boy chasing them. They ran around the school building twice, until Arthur stopped them. "What's going on?" Arthur demanded.

"There's a giant who's going to bite my ear off," Dwight told him.

Arthur peered over Dwight's shoulder. "Hey, Peters!" he shouted. "Why don't you pick on somebody your own size?"

"I was just kidding him," Peters said. "That's what we always do to the new kids."

"Well, you can do that with somebody else besides my brother," Arthur said. "If I ever see you near him again, I'll knock your block off."

"All right, all right," Peters said.

Dwight turned and watched Peters trot off to the other side of the playground. "Thanks, Arthur," he said.

"He really was probably just teasing you, Dwight," Arthur said, "but, in any case, you need to start fending for yourself."

"That's easy for you to say, Arthur, because you're bigger than Peters," Dwight said, "but he was twice my size."

"You know what they always say, Dwight," Arthur reminded him. "The bigger they are, the harder they fall."

For the next several weeks, Dwight thought about what Arthur had said. He wondered if he'd be able to hold his own against bigger competition. It wasn't long before he found out.

There was a boy in the eighth grade named Harvey Lyman, who was tall and heavyset and smelled, and nobody wanted to get near him. One day, Harvey had tied a large steel nut to a cord and was swinging it around his head. He stood at the front door of the school, daring anyone to touch him. Since the bell to end recess had just rung, everyone wanted to get to class, but nobody tried to pass by Harvey, for fear of what he might do.

Suddenly, out of nowhere, it seemed, Dwight rushed at Harvey. Dwight took him totally by surprise, causing Harvey to crash into the steps. Harvey was knocked unconscious.

Dwight took the cord with the steel nut out of Harvey's hands and pocketed it. He had decided that if Harvey ever tried to punish him for doing what he had just done, he'd have a weapon of Harvey's own creation to make sure it didn't happen.

When Harvey got out of the hospital, though, he didn't return to school. His family decided that Harvey was needed more on the farm than he was in the classroom. From that time on, whenever there was trouble on the school grounds, everyone always shouted, "Ike! Ike! Ike!" Now Dwight had the reputation of being one of the toughest kids in Abilene.

One time, though, Dwight's new image nearly got himself and his brother Edgar killed.

In May 1903, heavier than usual spring rains flooded most of the south side of Abilene, turning the streets into raging torrents. Still, Mrs. Eisenhower told Dwight and Edgar that they had to take their father's lunch to him at the creamery.

When they reached Buckeye Street, part of the wooden sidewalk was just starting to get caught up in the current.

"Let's get on it and float as far as the current takes us," Dwight suggested.

"All right," Edgar agreed.

Unfortunately, almost the entire south side of Abilene was now a tributary of the Smoky Hill River. Before Dwight realized it, the board they were on was going too fast for them to paddle to higher ground. At the last minute, they were saved by a man on horseback.

Their joy at being rescued was short-lived, though. When the man delivered them home, Mrs. Eisenhower broke one of her rules and whipped them.

The next day, when Dwight was recounting the story to Bob, Bob asked, "Did you learn a lesson from that?"

Dwight nodded. "Yes," he replied. "Never forget to take your father's lunch to him."

Burning Houses and Jail Breaks

The incident of the daring "rescue at sea" from the wooden sidewalk only further served to add to the Eisenhower boys' reputation that they were tough and willing to risk their lives for fun and excitement. Although there was nothing over the next year to top that adventure, both Dwight and Edgar managed to win enough fights, mostly against the north side boys, that no one even thought about challenging them for their titles.

By the end of summer, 1903, Edgar's reputation had actually surpassed Dwight's. A few months earlier, Edgar had beaten a larger north side opponent almost senseless just to claim that the south side was better.

In October, when Dwight had just turned thirteen, a tough north sider named Wesley Merrifield challenged Dwight to a fight, and Dwight accepted. He never even considered the possibility that he might lose.

When the time came for the fight, which was to be held in a vacant lot near the downtown area, it was clear that each boy would rather be doing something else.

It didn't matter what they thought, though, because a huge crowd had gathered, from both sides of Abilene, so both boys knew that a fight would have to take place.

When it started, Dwight rushed Wesley, and the two started pushing and shoving, raising their fists, but after an hour of this, one of the north siders broke it up, calling it a draw.

Both sides of the crowd howled that its

representative had won, but what they hadn't realized is that both Dwight and Wesley had whispered, almost simultaneously, to each other, "I can't lick you."

Dwight knew that nobody would ever know that, though, because he wasn't going to tell anyone, and he had the feeling that Wesley Merrifield wouldn't, either. In fact, if the social situation in Abilene had been different, Dwight decided on the way home, he and Wesley might even have become friends.

By evening, Dwight's left eye had swelled up and was turning black. There was no way he could hide the fight from his parents. At bedtime, when Mrs. Eisenhower came into the boys' room to tell them good night, she saw Dwight's eye and gave him a strong reprimand but ended his punishment for fighting at that.

When Dwight returned to school on Monday, one of the first people he saw was Wesley Merrifield, who was also sporting a black eye. Wesley gave him a big grin, but he didn't stop and talk.

In September 1904, Dwight entered Abilene High School. Unlike the elementary and junior high school, which were actually school buildings, the high school was in makeshift quarters on the second floor of the city hall downtown.

Dwight was disappointed. He had been looking forward to high school because, he had been told, north siders and south siders acted a little more civilized toward one another. Abilene High School didn't seem much like a school, but there were upsides to that, too.

The city jail and the quarters of the town fire marshal were on the first floor of the building, and all of the male students served as part of the volunteer fire department.

One morning, in early October, when Dwight and Edgar arrived at school, Dwight said, "Oh, I forgot to study for my English test. And I can't afford to fail it!"

But just as they headed into their classroom, the fire bell, situated in a cupola in one of the recitation rooms, rang to let everyone know there was a fire in town.

Right away, Dwight shouted, "I'll take the test tomorrow, Miss Johnson! We have to put out a fire now!"

Sometimes, if students were needed in class, as for an examination, teachers had the option of telling them they couldn't go, but Dwight made sure that Miss Johnson didn't have time to say anything. He immediately turned around and raced downstairs, followed by most of the other boys in the classroom, to where the horse-drawn fire engine was starting down the street.

The horse pulling the engine wasn't in the best of shape, so the boys were able to stay almost directly behind it as they headed into the north part of Abilene.

Finally, Dwight saw smoke over the tops of some trees.

"It's the Martins' house!" Edgar shouted.

Just then, Dwight saw Mrs. Martin come out the front door, pulling a large trunk behind her. Her face and dress were covered with soot, and her hair was hanging down in her eyes. The only other times Dwight had seen her, she had looked as if she had stepped off the pages of one of the women's magazines he had seen at Case's Department Store.

When Mrs. Martin saw the fire engine and the volunteers headed in her direction, she dropped the trunk and started running toward them.

"Help me save my dead baby's clothes," Mrs. Martin sobbed. "I can't let them burn up."

When no one else made a move to do anything, Dwight knew he had to act. "Where are they?" he asked Mrs. Martin.

124

"They're in the bedroom at the back of the house," Mrs. Martin said. "You'll find a trunk just like this one. Please save it for me."

To Dwight, it looked as if the fire was still confined to a front room. He didn't think there would be any problem making it to the room where the trunk was. When the other firemen started pumping water onto the fire, Dwight took off his shirt and tied it around his nose and mouth, then raced for the front door.

Inside, the house was filled with smoke, but not so much that Dwight couldn't see to maneuver through the rooms. As he did, he remembered the time when the Martin boys had told him to stay out of the neighborhood. Now, that seemed like a hundred years ago. Finally, Dwight found the back bedroom and saw the trunk Mrs. Martin had been talking about. He grabbed it by one of the leather handles and started pulling it out of the house.

Although the house had begun to fill up

with more smoke, Dwight could still see well enough to find the front door.

Outside, he dragged the trunk to the edge of the yard. Robert and John were now standing beside their mother and father. When they saw Dwight, they ran toward him.

"Thank you for doing that, Eisenhower," John said.

"It means a lot to our mother," Robert added.

Dwight nodded. "I'm glad I could do it for her," he said.

As Dwight put his shirt back on he watched Robert and John rejoin their parents, and he thought about how things had started to change, not only in his life, but in the life of Abilene.

Although Dwight and the rest of his classmates still wished they had a real high school to attend and could hardly wait until the new building was finished, they all agreed that life was never dull at Abilene High School.

• • •

One morning, several weeks after the fire at the Martins' house, Dwight arrived to see a group of his classmates standing outside the entrance. "What's going on?" Dwight called to them. "It's cold out here. Why isn't everyone inside?"

"You must be deaf, Eisenhower," someone said. "You didn't hear the explosion earlier this morning?"

Dwight shook his head. When he reached the knot of students, he saw what they were looking at.

A corner of the building had been dynamited away during an attempted jailbreak. The students were waiting for some of the debris to be cleared and for the sheriff and his deputies to make sure the upstairs part of the building was still safe for the students.

Just then, one of Dwight's teachers, Miss Stroehli, arrived, observed the scene, and said, "How the good citizens of Abilene think

I can teach you young people anything amidst the howling of dogs, the wailing of prisoners, and the odor of onions being cooked for the marshal's dinner, I do not know!"

Actually, Dwight thought, *I don't know, either, but somehow it's being done.*

A Matter of Life and Death

One Friday afternoon in the spring of 1905, when Dwight was fifteen, he and his friends Billy Stern and Johnny Whitsun were heading home from school.

To Dwight, spring had always meant baseball, but earlier in the day, one of the coaches had given them some surprise news. He told the three boys that, with their builds, they could all be track-and-field stars at Abilene High School. With just a little extra training, they could probably make it to the state championships in Topeka. That sounded good to Dwight.

Suddenly, Dwight said, "I'll race you two to the corner!"

"You're on, Eisenhower!" Billy and Johnny told him.

As they started down the wooden sidewalk, Dwight was in the lead until they reached the middle of the block. A loose board caught on the heel of Dwight's left shoe and caused him to fall. He could feel the rough wood tearing through the cloth of his pants and scraping his knee.

"Are you all right, Dwight?" Billy asked.

Dwight nodded and tried to put on a good face, but his knee felt as if it were on fire. What angered him the most, though, was that he had just bought the new pair of pants at Case's Department Store with money he had saved from selling vegetables the previous summer. He had wanted to have a really nice new pair for school so he would feel as though he fit in more with the north siders. He knew that very few of the students paid much attention to that anymore, since Dwight had become so popular at school. Still, it made him feel better about himself, and that was very important.

Johnny bent down and looked at Dwight's knee. "You scraped it pretty bad, Eisenhower, but it's not bleeding very much. You should be all right," he said.

"You two have obviously forgotten how tough I am," Dwight told them with a wide grin. "Something like this doesn't mean anything to an Eisenhower."

"Well, then, why are we worrying about you?" Billy said. He looked over at Johnny. "We probably should just leave him here on the sidewalk,"

Johnny pretended to think for a minute. "I don't know, Billy," he said. "He helped us with our Latin homework last night, so I guess we owe him this one."

They both offered Dwight their hands, but he waved them off. "I can get up by myself, fellows," he said.

As it turned out, though, the scrape caused Dwight so much pain that he had to limp the rest of the way home.

Dwight didn't say anything to his mother about his knee, but he did tell her that he had torn his new pants. He asked her if she would mind mending them for him.

When Mrs. Eisenhower noticed the blood on the cloth, she asked Dwight about it. He told her it was just a small scratch and that he was all right.

The next afternoon, Dwight's knee hurt him so much that it was almost impossible to walk. When he finally made it to his house, he went straight to his room, without saying a word to anyone, and lay down.

Arthur, Edgar, Roy, and Earl were so busy with their homework that they didn't notice. However, during the chores before supper, Edgar said, "Dwight was supposed to feed the chickens tonight, Mama, and he didn't do it."

"Are you sure?" Mrs. Eisenhower asked.

Edgar nodded. "When I passed the pen on my way back from milking the cows, the chickens were wandering all around, looking like they were trying to figure out what was wrong."

"Chickens are so dumb," Roy said. "Maybe they forgot they had already eaten."

Edgar shook his head. "I don't think so," he replied.

Just then, Earl came into the kitchen and said, "Who told Dwight he could go to bed instead of doing his chores?"

Mrs. Eisenhower looked at Earl, then at Roy, then finally at Edgar. "As ornery as Dwight can be sometimes, and that goes for the rest of you, too, he's never done anything like this before," she said. "You boys wash up for supper. I'll go see what the matter is."

Mrs. Eisenhower found Dwight lying on his bed, but he wasn't sleeping. Instead, he was thrashing around and moaning.

"Dwight," Mrs. Eisenhower said. "What's the matter?"

"I'm not going to swim across that muddy river," Dwight suddenly shouted. "It's full of mean squirrels who'll bite me!"

"Dwight!" Mrs. Eisenhower said. "You're not making any sense." She put her hand on his forehead. "Oh, my goodness, son, you're burning up with fever."

Mrs. Eisenhower ran downstairs, just as Mr. Eisenhower came in the front door. She told him that Dwight was very sick.

"I'll go get Dr. Conklin!" Arthur said.

"I'll go with you," Edgar said.

Mrs. Eisenhower hurried into the kitchen, got a couple of clean cloths from a cupboard, and said, "Roy, fill me a pan of cold water and bring it up, please!"

"All right, Mama!" Roy said. "Earl, you can help me!"

By the time Dr. Conklin finally arrived, Mrs. Eisenhower had bathed Dwight twice in the cold water, but his fever didn't seem to go down.

Mr. and Mrs. Eisenhower stood huddled together in the door of the boys' room while Dr. Conklin examined Dwight.

"Ah, now, here's the problem," Dr. Conklin finally said. He motioned for the Eisenhowers to come to the side of Dwight's bed. "This knee is infected!"

Mr. and Mrs. Eisenhower looked at Dwight's red, swollen knee.

"How did that happen?" Mr. Eisenhower asked.

"Dwight and some friends were running on one of those wooden sidewalks downtown, coming home from school yesterday," Mrs. Eisenhower said, "but he told me it was just a little scratch, and I didn't bother to look at it."

"He probably didn't clean it properly," Dr. Conklin said. "I'll douse it with some alcohol, and that should take care of it."

But it didn't.

Day after day, Dr. Conklin arrived to clean and re-dress the wound, but finally he said, "I'm afraid this is more serious than I had first thought, Mrs. Eisenhower. Dwight has blood poisoning, and if it gets into the rest of his body, we might not be able to save his life."

Mrs. Eisenhower gasped. "There must be something you can do, Doctor," she managed to say.

Dr. Conklin stood up. "I suggest that we amputate Dwight's leg," he said. "Cutting it off may be the only way to keep him alive."

Suddenly, Dwight started moaning loudly. He couldn't get any words out, but he was conscious enough to understand what Dr. Conklin had been saying. There was no way he'd let anybody cut off his leg.

"I just can't believe we would have to do that," Mrs. Eisenhower said. "I just can't believe it."

"I'm going to consult with another doctor,

Mrs. Eisenhower, so we won't do anything right away," Dr. Conklin said, "but if he agrees with me, then we'll need to perform the operation as soon as possible."

After Dr. Conklin left, Mrs. Eisenhower pulled a chair up next to Dwight's bed and resumed washing him with cold water. Suddenly, Dwight shouted, "I want Edgar! I want Edgar!"

At first, Mrs. Eisenhower thought Dwight was still delirious from the fever and that he didn't know what he was saying, but when he brushed her hand away from his face and repeated what he had said, she knew that he did. She hurried downstairs to get Edgar.

"Why would he want to see me, Mama?" Edgar asked. "He's my brother and I love him, but you know how Dwight and I can fight sometimes."

"Yes, I do know that, dear, all too well," Mrs. Eisenhower told him, "but he didn't ask for anyone else but you."

Edgar went upstairs to where Dwight was now struggling to sit up. "Here I am, Dwight," Edgar said softly. "What did you want?"

Dwight reached out, grabbed Edgar's hand, and pulled him closer to the bed. "The doctor wants to cut off my leg, Edgar," Dwight said with a raspy voice. "You can't let him do it."

"Oh, Dwight, you were just having a bad dream," Edgar assured him. "Nobody is going to do that."

"Edgar, you have to believe me, please, because I know what I heard," Dwight said. "I won't be able to play baseball or football or run track, and that's what I want to do in high school more than anything else in the world."

When Edgar didn't say anything, Dwight added, "You have to tell them, Edgar, you have to tell them. I know that I'm going to fall asleep, and I won't be able to." He lay back on his pillow and started sobbing. "I'd rather die than be a cripple."

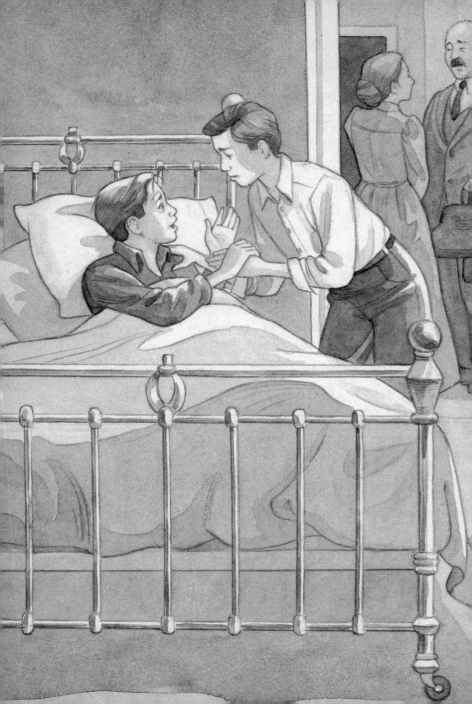

Finally, Edgar said, "I believe you, Dwight, and I promise you that I won't let them do it."

Edgar sat in the chair that Mrs. Eisenhower had been using and started wiping Dwight's face with the cloth.

When Mrs Eisenhower came back upstairs and told Edgar that she would take over Dwight's care, Edgar said, "No, Mama, I'm going to stay here. Dwight doesn't want the doctor to cut off his leg, so I'm not going to let him do it."

"It may not have to happen, Edgar," Mrs. Eisenhower assured him. "He's going to consult a doctor in Topeka, so we won't know anything until then."

"It doesn't matter," Edgar said. "It's not going to happen."

Edgar didn't leave Dwight's side all night. When morning came, Edgar quickly used the chamber pot, then he returned to the chair. Mrs. Eisenhower brought him something to eat. She tried to feed Dwight some broth, but he wouldn't take it.

About mid-morning, Dr. Conklin returned with a Dr. Smith from Topeka. Dr. Smith took one look at Dwight's leg and said, "Oh yes, yes, it must come off at once."

"No!" Edgar shouted. "Get out of here!"

"Edgar Newton Eisenhower!" Mrs. Eisenhower said. "You apologize to these gentlemen right this minute."

"I'm sorry I yelled," Edgar said, "but I promised Dwight that I wouldn't let anybody cut off his leg, and I'm going to keep my promise."

The two doctors turned to Mrs. Eisenhower.

"This is a very serious matter, Mrs. Eisenhower," Dr. Conklin said. "Your child could die if something isn't done soon."

Mrs. Eisenhower turned to look at Dwight. His eyes were open and they seemed to be on fire. His lips appeared to be forming words, but she couldn't hear anything he was saying. Finally, Mrs. Eisenhower looked at Dr. Conklin and Dr. Smith and said, "We need to pray about this first."

The two doctors nodded at her, then left the room.

By the next day, after everyone in the family had said several prayers asking for guidance in what should be done, Mrs. Eisenhower finally announced, "I think it is the Lord's will that Dwight's leg not be amputated, so I'm going to ask Dr. Conklin to continue treating Dwight as best he can without doing that."

Dr. Conkin agreed to do what he could.

Finally, the infection began to subside, and Dwight started to improve. But he remained in bed for the rest of the year, unable to return to school. He knew that when he finally did, though, he would able to play the sports that meant so much to him.

Intellectual Growth

From time to time, over the last few years, Edgar had occasionally dropped out of school to work. Even though Dwight had missed most of the previous year, he and Edgar were both in the same class when the new Abilene High School opened in the fall of 1907.

Since Edgar was already known as "Big Ike," Dwight let it be known that he would answer to "Little Ike," even though he was actually larger than his brother. Sometimes, several of Dwight's friends even called him

"Ugly Ike," which Dwight thought was funny.

After the first day of classes, as Dwight and Edgar were walking home, they passed the city hall. Dwight said, "I never thought I'd miss that place, but I do. I don't think we're going to have as much fun now."

Edgar nodded. "It's probably a good thing, because I guess we'd better start getting serious about our studies if we're going to college."

Dwight nodded.

Twenty-one-year-old Arthur had already left home to go to business school and was now working in Kansas City. Every time the family got a letter from him, he always began by telling Dwight and Edgar that it was important for them to go to college. Arthur even said he would help them with their tuition as much as he could.

Dwight knew that this was also the wish of his parents, even though there wasn't really any money available for it. He just assumed that his parents expected them to achieve this goal in the same way everything else was done in their family: through hard work, thrift, and personal responsibility.

One of the most exciting things about attending the new high school, Dwight discovered right away, was that they were able to begin everything from scratch. That included organizations, because none had existed before.

"We need an Abilene High School Athletic Association," Dwight told several of his friends before school one morning. "I'm going to ask the principal if we can have an organizational meeting in the auditorium after school."

"I have to work after school," George Franklin told him. "I can't come."

"I have to work, too, George," Dwight said. "I'll make sure the meeting doesn't last very long."

Dwight was true to this word. The meeting

only lasted a few minutes. Dwight had already written down exactly what he thought the organization should do, and everyone else agreed with him.

The new association would be made up of student athletes who would each pay twenty-five cents for dues, allowing the organization to provide uniforms, balls, and bats for the different teams. It was also decided to invite some of the local Abilene merchants to be honorary members, especially those who were interested in sports and who had the money to help buy the needed equipment.

"We'll need a president to run the organization," Happy Smith said. "I nominate Dwight Eisenhower, since this was all his idea."

Since everyone agreed with Happy, there was no need to take a vote.

The association not only attracted student athletes at the high school, but it was also very successful in getting support from local citizens.

For the merchants downtown, the success of the local high school athletes against the neighboring towns translated into a pride that allowed them to hold their heads up higher. Whenever one of the merchants happened to be visiting around the state and announced he was from Abilene, the first thing he often heard was, "You have a great football team over there," or, "That baseball team of yours could play with the big boys."

As for himself, Dwight had set his priorities early: sports, work, hunting, and studies. He didn't have a lot of time for girls, and that had disappointed more than one girl at Abilene High School. Although he didn't have a girlfriend, there were some girls from the south side of town he was still friends with, namely Ruby Norman, Gladys Harding, and Minnie Stewart. He had known them for most of his life, and he felt comfortable around them, mainly because they seemed more like sisters to him than girlfriends.

Once, when Gladys told him he should start dating, Dwight said, without any embarrassment, "I have no money, no clothes, and no time."

What he didn't tell Gladys was that he had actually asked a girl from the north side out on a date. When she had stood him up, he'd decided that he'd never do that again.

"I'm also a terrible dancer, Gladys," Dwight added.

"Oh, Dwight, that's not nearly as important as—" Gladys started to say.

Dwight stopped and looked at her. "As *what*?" he asked.

"Well, as the way you *look*," Gladys said.

"I can't help the way I look, Gladys," Dwight said testily.

"Oh yes, you can, Dwight David Eisenhower," Gladys said. "You can comb your hair and you can iron your clothes."

"None of my male friends complain about that," Dwight told her.

Gladys hit him playfully on the arm. "You're impossible," she said. She threw up her hands. "I guess you're just going to be a bachelor for the rest of your life."

Although Dwight liked most of his classes, he had little patience for teachers he thought shouldn't be in the classroom. He had the ability to remember everything he had ever read or that had been shown to him. He listened well, and he always asked the right questions. Sometimes he raised those questions not because he wanted to know the answers, which he already knew, but because he wanted to embarrass or humiliate the teacher.

"Why do you do that?" Edgar asked him once on the way home. "You only make it harder for me when I'm in their class."

"They aren't prepared to do their jobs, Edgar, that's why," Dwight responded. "They're supposed to be teaching me. I shouldn't have to teach them."

150

• • •

Dwight would also mark grades for his teachers in his schoolbooks. In them, he either wrote "good" or made a cross mark. One teacher he didn't like at all was Miss Gentry. She taught algebra, and he had given her a cross. It wasn't because of her personally, but because he detested algebra and seldom opened his textbook, even to study for a test. But Miss Gentry didn't like Dwight, either, because of his negative attitude toward her beloved subject. She seemed to enjoy giving him the lowest grades in the class.

It was the study of history that Dwight liked most. He idolized George Washington.

"He was brave and daring," he told the other students in his history class. "You should read his speeches sometime."

Of course, reading the speeches of a former president, even George Washington, didn't appeal to most of the students in his class. However, that didn't deter Dwight from continuing to lecture everyone, including the teacher, on Washington's military campaigns.

Dwight especially enjoyed ancient history, particularly that of the Greeks and the Romans. One of his heroes was Hannibal. He liked him not only for his military daring but for his understanding of the logistics of his times. Dwight read all he could about the "white hats"—the good people in history. Those included Julius Caesar, Socrates, Pericles, and Themistocles.

Their opposites, the "black hats," didn't escape Dwight's attention either. He also made a through study of Darius, Brutus, Xerxes, and Nero.

"Why would you want to read about *them*?" Minnie Stewart asked him one day.

"You need to know how your enemies think, Minnie," Dwight told her. "That's how you win battles."

A Born Leader

One of the things Dwight had been looking forward to most during his senior year in high school was football season. He loved the game and had absolutely no regard for his safety. This made him a much-feared player by school opponents. During their last season, Dwight played right-end and Edgar played fullback. But it wasn't just his physical prowess that other players counted on that fall, it was also his leadership ability.

As president of the athletic association, Dwight worked diligently, but he learned early on that pettiness among the members could undermine his efforts if he didn't deal with it right away. He easily met the challenge of handling a diverse group of individuals, both students and local merchants, most of whom had their own very definite ideas about how the association should work. Dwight even wrote a constitution, which he hoped would ensure the association's survival after he had graduated.

For the second game of the season, the team traveled to the nearby city of Salina, but right after they got there, Fred Stowers said, "Did you fellows know that Salina has a Negro halfback?"

Several of the players looked at one another and shook their heads in disbelief.

"Well, they do," Fred continued. "I saw him working out with the team when we drove in."

"How'd that happen?" Jonah Freeman asked. "They're not supposed to go to school with us, are they, Coach?"

Coach Bramstetter shrugged. "It just depends on the town, I guess," he told them.

"They should have told us about him before we came all this way," Karl Meers said.

"Why?" Dwight spoke up.

Karl looked at Dwight with a puzzled expression. "It's just not right, that's why," he said. "I'm not going to play if that Negro plays. I can tell you that for sure."

Several of the other players muttered their agreement.

Dwight pushed his way into the center of the dressing room. "That is no excuse for failing to play a game everyone expects us to play," he said. "If you fellows don't play this game tonight, then I'm going to quit the team."

Edgar stood next to Dwight to show his support.

"You can't do that, Eisenhower," Ben Jackson said. "You're one of our main players."

"We wouldn't have a team without you," Karl added.

"I mean it," Dwight told them. "We either play this game tonight, or I'll find something else to do on Friday nights."

Everyone finally agreed that the game should go on, although some of the players were still reluctant about it. To show he meant what he said, Dwight made a point of shaking hands with the Negro player both at the beginning of the game and at the end, after Abilene had won by a large margin.

That spring, Dwight wrote articles about athletics for the *Helianthus,* Abilene High School's yearbook. Under his senior class picture, the editor wrote that he was the best historian and mathematician in the graduating class. Edgar was described as the best football player. It was also customary for the editorial staff to publish class prophecies for each student. Agnes Curry, the editor, predicted that Edgar would be a future two-term president of the United States. Dwight, she had decided, would become a professor of history at Yale University.

Graduation night was May 27, 1909. The entire Eisenhower family, including Arthur, who had come in on the train from Kansas City, and Aunt Minnie and Uncle Luther, from Topeka, gathered in the school auditorium for the commencement exercises.

When Aunt Minnie saw Dwight, she said, "I can't believe this is the same young man who was chased by a goose in our pasture!"

Edgar looked at Dwight and grinned. "I haven't heard that story before, Aunt Minnie," he said.

Dwight punched Edgar playfully on the shoulder. "And you're not going to hear it now, either," he told him.

As Dwight and Edgar headed back out into the hallway to await the start of "Pomp and Circumstance," Dwight heard several of the sophomore and junior girls describing him to one another as "ruggedly handsome." He didn't know about that, he thought, but he did know that he was in pretty good shape. He was five feet eleven inches tall, weighed 145 pounds, and had been toughened by years of sports and hard, physical labor.

As Dwight stood in line, behind Edgar, marching slowly into the auditorium, he turned and looked back down the hallway once more and thought, *I'll always remember the good times here, but I'm ready to get on with my life.*

The next morning, Dwight awakened and realized that his future lay somewhere else besides Abilene. He had had a wonderful life there, but he didn't want to end up like his father, working in the local creamery for the rest of his life. He knew that the key to his future was, as Arthur had told him and Edgar, a college degree. The problem was finding the money for it.

"Well, first things first," Dwight said. He got out of bed and shook Edgar's shoulder.

"What's the matter?" Edgar asked sleepily.

"We're high school graduates now, brother," Dwight told him. "We can't expect our parents to take care of us anymore."

Edgar yawned. "Couldn't they give us just one more day of being a kid?" he asked.

Dwight shook his head. "No," he said. "If we're going to have enough money to go to college in the fall, we have to start working today."

Later that morning, after a good breakfast, Edgar went to work at the Belle Springs Creamery, and Dwight headed out to a farm owned by friends of Bob Davis.

West Point and World War I

Since the Eisenhower family couldn't afford college tuition for *both* Dwight and Edgar—even with Arthur's help—the two brothers agreed to work alternate years. That way, whichever brother was working could pay the fees of the one who was in school.

Since Edgar was older, it was decided that he should start college first. In the fall of 1909, Dwight took Edgar's job at the creamery where Mr. Eisenhower was employed and was able to send Edgar more than two hundred dollars. In 1910, Dwight found out from a friend that he would receive a free college education if he could get an appointment to the United States Military Academy at West Point, New York. Dwight had no particular interest in becoming a soldier, but this was an opportunity too good to pass up. Dwight studied hard for the very competitive West Point entrance exam, and in 1911 he won an appointment.

Although Dwight was only an average student at West Point, he excelled in sports. But that all changed when a knee injury forced him to quit the football team. Dwight was so devastated by the event that he almost left West Point, but his roommate convinced him to stay and finish his education. Dwight graduated in 1915, ranking sixty-first in a class of 164 men.

Dwight's first assignment as a new army officer was at Fort Sam Houston, in San Antonio, Texas. Not long after he arrived, he met Mamie Geneva Doud. Dwight knew almost immediately that he wanted her to become his wife, but Mamie's father didn't want his daughter to marry a soldier. Despite her father's concerns, when Dwight proposed to Mamie, she said yes. They were married on July 1, 1916. They eventually had two sons: Doud Dwight, who died in childhood, and John.

In 1917, when the United States entered World War I, Dwight was promoted to the rank of captain. He applied for a combat assignment overseas, but he was turned down. His superior officers valued him so much that they put him in command of Camp Colt, at Gettysburg, Pennsylvania. It was his job to train the fighting unit of one of the army's first tank corps.

What Dwight really still wanted, though, was a combat assignment. In October 1918, he finally received orders to take the tanks to France, but the war ended before his outfit could sail. Still, Dwight was decorated for his

163

service and promoted to lieutenant-colonel for his accomplishments in commanding the tank corps training center.

Between World War I and World War II, Dwight was recognized as one of the most promising instructors at the Command and General Staff School (CGSS), where soldiers went for officer training.

Dwight also served as an industrial mobilization planner. Although the United States was not yet involved in a war, there was concern that it soon would be. Dwight's job was to help get American companies ready for it.

After that, Dwight became an aide to General Douglas MacArthur, who not only was chief of staff of the United States Army but also field marshal of the Philippine Army, having been appointed to that post by President Manuel L. Quezon.

World War II

World War II began in Europe in 1939, when Nazi Germany invaded Poland. Most Americans knew that it was probably just a matter of time before the United States would be involved.

During various military training exercises in the period from 1940 through 1941, Dwight held several army staff positions and received much praise. This resulted in his becoming Chief of Staff of the Third Army, responsible for the army troops stationed in the United States. At the same time, Dwight was also promoted to brigadier general, the lowest general rank in the United States Army.

After the Japanese attacks on Pearl Harbor, Hawaii, and the Philippines, the United States entered World War II. Dwight was assigned to the War Department because of his expert knowledge of that area of the world. Three months later, he was promoted to major general because of the excellent job he did.

In June 1942, Dwight was given command of the United States forces in Europe. He would be leading them in the fight against Germany. Dwight was in charge during the successful invasions of North Africa, Sicily, and Italy in 1943. Once again, he demonstrated his excellent military skills.

In December 1943, Dwight was appointed Supreme Commander of the Allied Expeditionary Force for the invasion of France. This force was made up of armies from all of

the countries around the world that were fighting against the Nazis. Dwight was now a full general. He made all of the crucial decisions on D-day, the day of the Allied assault, June 6, 1944.

On December 15, 1944, Dwight became general of the U.S. Army. Now he was responsible for a force of almost 5 million troops. However, the next day, Germany began its last offensive in the Ardennes highlands of Belgium, catching the Allies by surprise. American troops were badly outnumbered and were forced to retreat. Because of bad weather, the Allied air force was unable to help. The deep German penetration created a bulge in the Allied lines. This gave the battle its name: the Battle of the Bulge. Dwight's decision that all of the armies should advance more or less at the same time toward Germany caused a disagreement with the commander of the British forces, Field Marshal Bernard Law

Montgomery. He favored concentrating the attacks in one area, which Dwight thought was too risky. Using his knowledge and experience, combined with the charm and tact he had developed back in Abilene, Dwight prevailed.

On May 7, 1945, the Germans surrendered unconditionally at Dwight's headquarters in Reims, France.

In the fall of 1945, Dwight became Army Chief of Staff. He served in that capacity for more than two years. During that time, he had the dual role of helping military troops return to civilian life and maintaining a suitable defense force for peacetime. Dwight also wrote his memoirs, *Crusade in Europe.*

In 1948, to the surprise of many, Dwight was offered the presidency of Columbia University, in New York City, and he accepted. Now, people who had never before heard of the university became quite familiar with it. But Dwight also continued to serve as a military adviser to the American government.

In early 1950, President Harry Truman named Dwight to command the troops of the North Atlantic Treaty Organization (NATO), an organization of nations pledged to stop any advance into Western Europe by the Soviet Union and its allies. Unfortunately, Dwight had only limited success. First of all, the Europeans were still recovering from the destruction of the war and were unable to raise new armies. Then, in June of that year, American troops were diverted to South Korea when Communist North Korea invaded it, starting the Korean War.

President of the
United States

Although Dwight had previously turned down several requests from both the Democratic and Republican parties to run for the presidency, he was finally persuaded to be the Republican candidate during the presidential campaign of 1952. As an enormously popular war hero, he also appealed to a lot of Democrats and easily defeated their candidate, Adlai Stevenson, by almost 7 million votes.

On domestic issues, President Eisenhower stood for things that appealed to many

Americans. He thought that big government was dangerous. He tried to limit its role in the lives of Americans, but he was also known for expanding the Social Security program, giving aid to education, and starting the Interstate Highway system.

Although President Eisenhower was criticized for his failure to oppose Senator Joseph McCarthy's ruthless search for Communists in the United States government and for his lack of support for the emerging civil rights movement, his supporters pointed out that McCarthyism collapsed without presidential intervention and that President Eisenhower did send federal troops to Little Rock in 1957 to enforce school integration.

In foreign matters, President Eisenhower took a particular interest in military and diplomatic affairs. He breathed new life into the National Security Council and quickly ended the Korean War on July 27, 1953.

When President Eisenhower reduced the

size and strength of the conventional military force, though, and sought instead to emphasize air power, he met resistance from many of his fellow army officers.

Even though there were some temporary thaws in the Cold War during President Eisenhower's years in office, the struggle with the Soviet Union continued. President Eisenhower fully supported his moralistic, anti-Communist, secretary of state, John Foster Dulles, who often threatened war to gain diplomatic ends, but President Eisenhower did not intervene militarily in Vietnam to save the French in 1954, or during the Hungarian revolt against the Soviet Union in 1956.

Soviet threats around the world, as well as the technological and psychological coup of launching Sputnik, the first artificial satellite, in October 1957, drew only a typically cautious response from him.

In 1960, when President Eisenhower went

on national television to accept full responsibility for a U-2 plane's spy flight over the Soviet Union, all hopes were dashed for any kind of peaceful relations with the Communist world.

When President Eisenhower left office in 1961, he and Mamie retired to a small farm they owned outside Gettysburg, Pennsylvania, an area Dwight had loved ever since he had been stationed there during World War I. Former high school classmates visiting from Abilene reminded Dwight of the senior class prophecy that his brother Edgar would serve two terms as president of the United States and that Dwight would be a history professor at Yale. Everyone had a good laugh over that.

During the winter months, Dwight and Mamie lived in Palm Desert, California, where Dwight played golf.

Dwight wrote a two-volume history of his presidency entitled *The White House Years*.

He also wrote a personal memoir called *At Ease: Stories I Tell to Friends.*

Dwight was also still involved in politics. President Kennedy and later President Johnson asked him for his advice on various matters.

In 1964, Dwight endorsed Republican presidential candidate Barry Goldwater, who lost, and in 1968, he supported his former vice president, Richard Nixon, who won. That same year, Dwight and Mamie's grandson, David, married Nixon's daughter Julie.

Dwight's health began to fail in 1965, and over the next few years he suffered several heart attacks. He spent the last few months of his life at Walter Reed Army Medical Center, in Washington, D.C.

On March 28, 1969, the day Dwight died, he said, "I've always loved my wife. I've always loved my children. I've always loved my grandchildren. And I've always loved my country. I want to go. God take me."

For More Information

BOOKS

Ambrose, Stephen E. *Eisenhower: Soldier and President.* New York: Simon & Schuster, 1990.

D'Este, Carlo. *Eisenhower: A Soldier's Life.* New York: Henry Holt and Company, 2002.

WEB SITE

http://www.eisenhower.archives.gov
This is the official Web site of the Dwight D. Eisenhower Presidential Library, in Abilene, Kansas.

CHRISTOPHER COLUMBUS

ANNE FRANK

DIANA, PRINCESS OF WALES

POPE JOHN PAUL II

LEONARDO DA VINCI

MOTHER TERESA

COMING SOON:

GANDHI

★ ★ COLLECT THEM ALL! ★ ★